At the sound of hoofbeats, they both looked toward the road.

"It's your folks," Susannah murmured.

Jethro nodded, recognizing his *daed*'s horse. "*Gut* thing I'm here then. Support the news I'm sure they've heard around the d-district that we're courting."

"Have they said anything to you yet?"

"*Nee.* B-but I'm sure it's coming soon. You?"

"*Nee.* Unlike you, I don't think they'll speak directly to me about it. I think it's more likely that the bishop will just send more 'eligible' men my way." She bumped him with her hip. "Thanks to your idea about the courtship that's not a courtship, when I say thanks but no thanks, most of them will be easily dissuaded."

At the sight of her teasing grin, it was Jethro's feet—not his speech for once—that stumbled. "Glad it's working out for you."

Watching the buggy crest the hill and drop from sight, Jethro cautioned himself with Susannah's words. *She doesn't want a beau. And even if she did, I wouldn't be on her list of potential candidates.* He needed to keep his heart in check.

Publishers Weekly bestselling author
Jocelyn McClay grew up on an Iowa farm,
ultimately pursuing a degree in agriculture. She
met her husband while weight lifting in a small
town—he "spotted" her. After thirty years in
business management, they moved to an acreage
in southeastern Missouri to be closer to family
when their oldest of three daughters made them
grandparents. When not writing, she keeps
busy grandparenting, hiking, biking, gardening,
quilting, knitting and substitute teaching.

Books by Jocelyn McClay

Love Inspired

The Amish Bachelor's Choice
Amish Reckoning
Her Forbidden Amish Love
Their Surprise Amish Marriage
Their Unpredictable Path

Visit the Author Profile page at LoveInspired.com.

Their
Unpredictable
Path

Jocelyn McClay

LOVE INSPIRED
INSPIRATIONAL ROMANCE

LOVE INSPIRED®
INSPIRATIONAL ROMANCE

Recycling programs for this product may not exist in your area.

ISBN-13: 978-1-335-56755-0

Their Unpredictable Path

Love Inspired
22 Adelaide St. West, 41st Floor
Toronto, Ontario M5H 4E3, Canada
www.LoveInspired.com

Printed in U.S.A.

But the Lord said unto Samuel,
Look not on his countenance, or on the height
of his stature; because I have refused him:
for the Lord seeth not as man seeth;
for man looketh on the outward appearance,
but the Lord looketh on the heart.
—*1 Samuel* 16:7

Again, and always, I thank God for this opportunity. I want to thank Denise for letting me feed her goats, Lorelle for her wise character insight and Anthony for sharing how it feels to run toward a fire. In addition, I thank Mitch for information on clefts, Kim for responding to my questions on stuttering and SLP professionals for the difference they make in many lives. Moriah, this one's for you.

Chapter One

This time, he wasn't going to do it. No matter the pressure they applied. Jethro Weaver sighed and wearily shook his head. And his father, the bishop, and strong-willed mother could certainly apply considerable amounts. Turning out of his folks' lane, he gave a gentle *click* of his tongue to urge his gelding to road speed.

Ever since his wife and unborn child had unexpectedly died the previous year, his parents had been encouraging—Jethro's mouth slanted at the delicate term given the flat-out directives the bishop and his wife used—him to remarry. He loved his parents and wanted to obey them. He even understood their motive was pure. They wanted him to have a family. Large families were a gift from *Gott*. Jethro agreed.

But maybe it was a gift he wasn't meant to receive.

Maybe it didn't go with the other gifts he'd been given. The cleft lip and palate that had startled his parents when he'd been born. The stutter that frustrated him almost every time he opened his mouth, making him self-conscious around folks. Particularly around women.

Nee, going courting was the last thing he wanted to do.

His hands lax on the lines, Jethro let the gelding take his time as they started up a long hill, part of the rolling countryside in this slice of Wisconsin. It'd been different when he'd married Louisa. There'd been no courtship. He'd married the shy, frail widow of his younger brother to take care of her. *Ja,* it'd been at his parents' urging, but he'd have eventually done it on his own as she'd needed help.

Jethro slumped on the buggy seat. Although he usually succumbed to his parents' wishes, due in part to his respect for them and to his father's position as bishop of their district, he didn't relish the coming battle of wills. Because this time he wasn't going to do it. Why couldn't they let him live his life as he saw fit?

At the sudden pricked-forward ears of his gelding, Jethro glanced up the road. A battle was indeed erupting before him. Farther up the hill, a buggy was swerving perilously close to the ditch as the horse pulling it shied and reared. Jethro straightened abruptly when the animal lost its footing and tumbled over, flipping the buggy down the incline as well. At his urgent command, his startled gelding lurched ahead.

The horse swerved and reared. The lines jerked through Susannah Mast's fingers as the buggy jolted toward the ditch. She struggled to recapture the lost leather as Amos slid across the tilted seat toward her.

"Mamm!" Her eleven-year-old son's voice was high with alarm. "What's wrong with Nutmeg?"

Shoulder braced against his pressuring weight, Susannah didn't have an answer as to why their normally placid mare was suddenly shying and lunging out of control. Usually steadfast in harness, the Standardbred had been fidgety and reluctant to pull today. But it wasn't until she'd started climbing the hill toward home that Nutmeg had gone completely berserk.

"Easy, girl! Easy!" It was useless. Susannah had no control. Even as she regained the slack in the lines and struggled to settle the mare to a stop, Nutmeg fought her. Flecks of foam flew from the mare's flinging head as she hurled herself farther into the long, dried grass of the steep ditch.

A crack of fracturing wood, along with the horse's shrill whinny, split the previous quiet of the autumn afternoon. Susannah's shriek as the rearing mare toppled over the now broken buggy shaft joined it. The buggy lifted beneath her. Dropping the lines, Susannah twisted to wrap her arms around her son. Amos's straw hat went flying as she jerked him to her chest. Hunching her shoulders, she dipped her head over his, striving to protect him as the world tumbled around them.

Wincing, Susannah tightened her grasp when the edge of the buggy—door-less on the sunny October day—slammed into her back. *Please, Gott, don't let the buggy roll over on us.* Something pelted the top of her head, jerking at the pins that secured her *kapp*. A grunt escaped her, along with her breath, as her shoulder drove into the ground. Squeezing her eyes shut, she hugged her son.

One by one, Susannah's senses finally stopped whirling. Her nose was pressed against her son's head; she could smell in his hair the leather and straw of his new hat along with the haylike aroma of recently broken vegetation.

A wheel squeaked as it continued to spin. At the sound of her mare thrashing in the ditch, Susannah's eyes popped open. Loosening her arms from around Amos, she capped his shoulders with her hands and carefully eased him back a few inches. His youthful face was pale, his freckles showing in sharp contrast. When he opened his eyes, they went instantly wide, the dark blue irises riveted on her.

"Are you all right?" she demanded, barely refraining from hugging him to her again.

"Ja." The word was hesitant and drawn out, almost a question in itself. "I think so?"

Praise Gott! Susannah slumped against the crumpled grass in relief as she ran a hand through his hatless dark hair. Scanning his small frame, she checked for signs of blood or possible injuries as he slowly shifted upright and away from where she sprawled. Her frantic heart rate began to ebb. Wincing at the pain in her shoulder, Susannah pushed herself into a sitting position. She was framed in the doorway of the upended buggy. Scattered around her were loose contents of the rig's interior.

The mare whinnied in distress. The horse's flailing had ceased, but the mare's labored breathing was evident. "I have to get to Nutmeg. Can you stand?"

Amos's nod was more emphatic this time.

"Ja." They both froze when the buggy groaned, followed by a rocking sway, threatening it could tip further. They had to get out. Susannah's gaze darted across the toppled interior. Over the dash and out the open front was their best option. But should the mare begin to thrash again, they'd be within reach of flailing hooves. Though uninjured now, a kick to the head or limb would quickly change that.

At a distinct holler from the road, her heart stuttered. Twisting, Susannah looked through the buggy's open front to see Jethro Weaver scrambling down the ditch. She almost sank back to the ground in relief at the sight. Having tended to her neighbor's young son while in her preteen years, she'd known the calm and steady man all his life.

"We're all right!" She waved him away as he approached the buggy. "Check on Nutmeg!"

With an acknowledging wave, he reversed direction and more cautiously advanced to where the horse was trying to lift her head. When he settled on his haunches beside the Standardbred, Susannah heard his indistinct murmuring as he stroked the horse's neck. The old mare quieted.

Susannah struggled upright and eased into the overturned buggy. Keeping a wary eye on Nutmeg's hind feet, she hovered against the dash with Amos at her side. Jethro nodded to her as he continued to soothe and distract the mare.

"Follow me," Susannah murmured to her son. With a shaky inhale, she climbed over the dash. Using the frame of the buggy for support, she edged away from the overturned rig and clear of the metal-shod hooves before turning to watch anxiously as Amos did the same.

When they were both out of the range of danger, she gave her son another quick hug before kneeling beside Jethro at the mare's head. Nutmeg's eyes were ringed with white. In spite of the temperate October day, sweat darkened her brown neck. Susannah cooed to the mare as she ran her hand down the slick surface.

"Is she hurt?" Her gaze locked on Jethro's blue eyes, trying to decipher the concern visible there.

"D-don't know yet. Let's see." Jethro rose to his feet. Continuing to soothe the mare, Susannah watched as he worked his way down the buggy's shaft that jutted above the prone horse. His tall frame bent over the mare, the lean muscles of his forearms visible below the rolled-up sleeves of his white shirt as he efficiently unfastened the buckles and straps of the harness.

Squatting to gently rest a hand on Nutmeg's side so she knew he was there, Jethro considered the shaft and the harness leather that tracked under the mare. Tipping his flat-brimmed straw hat farther back over his sandy-blond hair, he glanced toward Susannah. Above his short beard, his lips were pressed into a pensive line, making the white scar that ran from under his nose to the top one stand out in his tanned face.

Susannah interpreted his dilemma. "I don't care about the harness or the buggy. I just want to help Nutmeg."

Nodding, Jethro set about doing what was necessary to free the mare. By the time he returned to where Susannah knelt, both she and the mare were breathing more easily.

"Let's t-try it now." With a hand at her elbow, Jethro helped Susannah to her feet. "Stand b-back," he directed her and the hovering Amos before grabbing the mare's bridle.

Susannah couldn't hear what he was saying but she knew the mare was listening as her brown ears flicked back and forth. Susannah pulled Amos in front of her, her hands tightening on his slender shoulders as she anxiously watched Jethro guide the mare into a position to rise. With Jethro's encouragement, the horse struggled to lunge to her feet. At each attempt,

Susannah pushed herself onto her toes as if she could help man and horse by doing so. By the time Nutmeg staggered to a stand on the third try, Susannah was shaking as much as the horse. Scanning her side of the mare for any obvious injuries, she hurried to the trembling Standardbred.

"Careful, in case she goes d-down again," Jethro cautioned. Biting her lip, Susannah nodded as she grasped the bridle, freeing Jethro to examine the animal.

"Her legs look good," she observed in relief. There was no response from Jethro, who was making his way along the far side of the horse. Fretting for reassuring feedback, Susannah prompted, "Don't they?"

"Ja."

She could almost hear a reluctant smile in his voice. Susannah took it as encouragement.

After a moment's pause, Jethro continued in a more serious tone. "She seems all right. Won't know for sure until she walks. B-but she's b-bleeding a b-bit on this side. Looks like it's coming from under the collar."

"Bleeding!" Susannah scooted around the front of the mare to see a red stain running down the mare's shoulder. As Jethro had noted, the inception point was under the leather collar that circled her lower neck. "Let's get this off."

Her fingers fumbled in their efforts to unhook the few remaining attachments. Jethro's tanned fingers gently brushed hers aside. Quickly finishing the task, he carefully lifted the collar from the mare to reveal a small gash sullenly seeping blood.

"Poor dear," Susannah murmured as she gently explored the wound. "Why there, of all places?"

Jethro was quietly examining the collar when she felt an abrupt tension charge his lean figure. When he spoke, his voice was tight. "B-because of this." Shifting the collar so she could see, he pointed to the head of a nail protruding from its interior. "Although it would've fretted her while d-driving earlier, climbing the hill t-to your p-place d-did the d-damage."

Jaw sagging, Susannah blinked in astonishment at the bloodstained nail. "How…" she said faintly before her teeth clamped together. She knew how.

"Let's see how she m-moves." Leaning the collar against the dash of the upturned buggy, Jethro gathered up the abandoned lines in one hand as he returned to Nutmeg's head. He took a firm grip of the bridle with his other to support the horse. Sharing a tense glance with Susannah, he gently coaxed the mare forward. Nutmeg reluctantly took one step, then two before slowly walking by Jethro's side along the waving autumn-golden grass in the ditch's belly.

There was no hitch in the horse's gait nor was she bobbing her head as she walked, either of which might indicate an injury. Susannah sighed in relief. Catching up to where Jethro had drawn Nutmeg to a halt, she threw her arms around the mare's neck and pressed her face against the black mane. "No limp. Praise *Gott* you're not hurt!"

Leaning back, she looked over her shoulder at the overturned buggy. Susannah's joy evaporated as her stomach clenched. Delayed reaction and overwhelming relief that Amos and the mare were safe almost made her sick. Her nose prickled with the threat of tears. Withdrawing her arms from the mare, Susannah curled her hands into fists. She blinked any renegade tears from her eyes as the sting of fingernails pressing into her palms helped her retain her equilibrium. She would not cry. Very few people had ever seen her cry. Susannah knew some wondered if she even could.

Her shock from the accident fading, the twinges and pains incurred in the tumble now made themselves known. Her shoulder throbbed. Her knee must've slammed against the dashboard. Her scalp was tender from whatever had pelted it.

Worst of all was her heart. Her heart ached. For she knew who was responsible for the dreadful incident. All evidence pointed to her hired man. What she didn't know was why. But she would find out.

She needed to fire him. And she dreaded that for many reasons, one of which was that releasing the young man would compound her issues. Lack of a hired hand would just give the bishop another reason to prompt her to remarry. He didn't think she could run the farm by herself. It wasn't like she hadn't run it alone before. But a widow with a prosperous farm was tempting for the ambitious—as well as the not so ambitious—older single men in the community, some of whom she knew had been bending the bishop's ear. Their unwanted courtships were the last thing she wanted or had time for.

"Oh, John, why did you do this? For your circumstances as well as my own." Because as much as she needed a worker, her hired man needed a job. Susannah could've dealt with his recent slothfulness. But when he harmed her animals, he had to go, no matter what that did to her own situation.

* * *

Jethro watched Susannah's brown eyes migrate from a wide-eyed dismay to a narrowed-lidded intensity. The focused ferocity of her gaze contrasted with the disarray of the rest of her appearance. A crushed prayer *kapp* hung off the side of her head, clinging precariously by a few dislodged pins. Dark brown hair, threaded with very little gray to share a clue to her age, dangled from a tangle at the back of her head. One lock had escaped completely to trail behind her shoulder to her waist.

His own eyes widened. Although he'd witnessed Susannah working hard in the fields or even hopping mad, he'd never seen her so... disheveled. Or with her hair even partially down. The only Amish woman he'd seen with her hair down had been his deceased wife, and those occasions had been rare and far between. Jethro's gaze lingered on the dangling strand where the autumn sun glowed on a few strands of red in the thick tress. The corner of his lip twitched. Somehow, the discovery didn't surprise him. Much to his delight as a shy only child for several years, he'd found Susannah a babysitter willing to be adventuresome. She'd scrambled up many trees and waded in muddy creeks in his wake, or he in hers.

But it also didn't concern him. Jethro tactfully redirected his gaze to the mare. Susannah was a neighbor and friend, nothing more. A friend who currently needed his help. Not his ogling of her partially unbound hair. That sight should be reserved for a woman's husband. And from what he'd overheard today between his parents, Susannah would soon have one of those if it were up to the bishop and his wife.

He sighed. From what he knew of Susannah, she didn't want to remarry any more than he did. They were both in a similar situation. Jethro reached out to comb his fingers through the mare's mane, freeing tangles in the coarse black strands before patting Nutmeg's dark brown neck. Too bad his and Susannah's tangles couldn't be addressed as easily. If only they could help one another with the snarls that others strove to create for them.

Jethro stilled, his eyes stared unseeing at the mane before him as a possibility struck. Heart pounding, he darted a glance at Susannah. Would she think the scheme blooming in his head *narrish*, or would the crazy thing be not to take action on the idea when it could be the solution, at least temporarily, for both their problems? He forced a swallow down a suddenly dry throat. There was one way to find out.

Jethro turned to the hovering boy. "Amos,

could you d-drive m-my rig t-to your house?"
The Mast farm was less than a quarter mile
distant. Nodding eagerly, Amos scrambled up
the ditch and into Jethro's buggy. A moment
later, the *clip-clop* of hooves on the blacktop
echoed behind the departing buggy, its cadence slow in comparison to Jethro's pulse.

He loved his parents, but it was time they
let him run his own life. If they wanted him
to go courting, so be it. But if the woman he
walked out with was someone they'd think unsuitable, a widow at least ten years his senior
and one toward the end of her childbearing
years who couldn't give him the large family
they—not he—wanted… Maybe they'd finally
leave him alone. Jethro's mouth curved into a
broad smile as an enthusiasm he hadn't felt in
a long time unfurled inside him.

He considered again the woman beside him,
the only female he'd ever felt comfortable with.
If only Susannah would agree to his plan…

His shoulders sagged as he took in Susannah's pale face and disheveled appearance.
He couldn't ask her now. She was still shaken
from the buggy accident. Having already had
one woman in his life who'd regretted her acceptance of his proposal, he didn't want Susannah to be the second, even for a fictional
relationship.

Jethro rubbed the back of his neck. Besides, how was he to broach the plan convincingly, even at an appropriate time, when he occasionally struggled to get through a sentence? Although tempted to send a prayer on the matter, he didn't, knowing the scheme was his will, not *Gott's*. Pivoting to contemplate his folks' farmstead a large field's distance away, Jethro grimaced at the pressure he knew would soon come to bear from them.

The mare bobbed her head. Jethro turned back, his gaze pausing on the upturned buggy. First things first. Right now, Susannah had more pressing needs than a proposed fake relationship to an unsuitable partner.

"When we get your mare t-to the b-barn, I'll b-bring my horse b-back and pull your b-buggy out. One in the d-ditch is b-bad enough. One t-tipped would p-put folks in a t-t-tizzy." Jethro closed his eyes in frustration as he finally got the word out. At the touch of a hand on his arm, he opened them to meet Susannah's warm gaze.

"*Denki*, Jethro. I don't know how to thank you."

He smiled slightly. He hoped she'd remember that when he had the courage to propose his plan.

"You'd have d-done the same for me."

"*Ja.* But not as well." When Susannah removed her hand from his arm, the fallen lock of her hair slipped from behind her shoulder to slide into view. She glanced at it in confusion before hastily reaching up to touch the disarray of her hair and *kapp*.

A flush crept up her cheeks. Rescuing the *kapp* from its precarious perch, she tucked the pins between her lips as she corralled her escaped hair. With deft fingers, she swiftly secured the dark tresses. Quickly reshaping the dented *kapp*, she repinned the prayer covering over her now neatly coiled hair.

Giving her some privacy to put herself to rights, Jethro turned toward the road. Far down its dark surface, he could see a rig coming their way. "When I get your b-buggy t-to your p-place, I'll check over the d-damage. If it's something I can fix, I'll t-take care of it t-tomorrow." His offer had nothing to do with what he was hoping she'd agree to. It was an automatic response to a neighbor in need.

"I couldn't ask you to do that."

"You d-didn't. I offered."

"Well, the least I could do then is fix you some dinner."

"That's all right. I'll b-be fine." They were surely some of the fastest words he'd ever gotten out. Susannah was known in the district for her cooking, and not in a good way.

He glanced at her to ensure his hasty words hadn't offended. Susannah's brown eyes had lost their worry. She grinned. "Coward," she teased.

"P-probably. Or m-maybe just careful." He tugged the mare forward. By tacit agreement, Susannah fell in step beside the horse as he gingerly led Nutmeg out of the steep ditch to the blacktop.

As they started up the road toward the Mast farm, Jethro was aware that every step he took shortened the opportunity for a private conversation. To put his plan into motion and head off the queue of women his parents would soon push in his direction, he needed to secure Susannah's participation. The leather in his hands grew damp as his palms began to sweat. Jethro scowled. Maybe he was a coward. Surely facing Susannah on the question of a fabricated courtship was much better than confronting a continuous sequence of the district's single women who'd be looking for a real one. Hoping for some type of inspiration, he opened his mouth, only to close it again at the sound of an approaching horse and buggy.

Susannah winced as she looked behind them. "What is it?" Immediately concerned, Jethro stopped the mare. Injuries didn't always make themselves initially known. Susannah may have been more harmed in the accident than she'd let on. "Are you hurt?"

"*Ach, nee.* But my ears will when he comes calling." She nodded toward the approaching rig. "Which will unfortunately be in the next day or so." Susannah slanted Jethro an unhappy look. "At least, according to the bishop."

Jethro's heart began thrumming in his ears, loud enough to drown out the *clip-clop* of the oncoming hooves on the blacktop as he watched Leroy Albrecht, a widower in the district, bear down on them. Maybe *Gott* didn't mind getting on board with Jethro's plan after all. He'd just provided a window of opportunity, one perhaps open wide enough for Jethro to clumsily wiggle through.

"Sounds like we are in a similar situation." He turned to where Leroy was drawing his horse to a halt beside them.

"Everything all right?" the portly man called through the open buggy door.

"Just fine!" chirped Susannah. "Just a little mishap that tipped us into the ditch. But we're all fine."

The man shifted to look back at the listed buggy. "Yours, Susannah? I would think you'd be a better driver at your age. Surely you know how to handle a fractious horse? I suppose I could teach you, should you have any aptitude for horsemanship."

Although Jethro heard Susannah's teeth snap together, he didn't think the sound had carried to the man in the buggy. He snuck a glance at Susannah. Her face—pale after the accident—was now as red as the late-season tomatoes in his garden.

"*Denki* for the offer, Leroy. She got away from me today when a…bee stung her, but we always get along otherwise just fine." Jethro wondered how Susannah got the words out through her gritted teeth.

"Well, should you need a lesson, you remind me when I come over. Day after tomorrow, *ja*?"

"*Ja*. So the bishop had mentioned. That's just…fine." The final word was said as if its meaning was something entirely different from the word that was spoken.

Leroy merely nodded as he lifted the lines. "See you then."

Jethro returned the man's parting wave before raising an eyebrow at his companion. "That was quite a 'fine' visit."

Susannah closed her eyes in a give-me-patience look. "*Ach*, it would be fine if no one would bother me. The last thing I want or need right now is to have unwanted visitors come courting. I'm busy enough, especially now with having to—" She bit off what she was going to say, instead reaching to carefully stroke the mare above the bloodstain on her dark brown neck. "Any reasonable candidates would be too busy finishing fall work to go courting now."

"Leaving the unreasonable ones t-to show up?" Too nervous to stand still in case he botched this unexpected opportunity, Jethro gently urged the mare forward. "What if... something came up t-to keep them away? At least until after harvest?" he hastily added.

"That would be *wunderbar*." There was a heartfelt sigh from the other side of the mare where Susannah now walked. "Do you think you could persuade your *daed* that any court-ship should wait until the winter? Or never?"

Jethro bit his upper lip, worrying the sec-tion below the surgery scar where he had no feeling. This wasn't going in the direction he'd hoped. "Ah, *nee*. It's d-difficult t-to p-persuade m-my *d-daed* about m-much of anything." He winced as he struggled over the words. "I was thinking of p-proposing—" Jethro cringed. That definitely wasn't the word he'd wanted to use. "I was thinking of an alternative. One that could help b-both of us."

"That sounds extremely tempting. Anything does to avoid having a parade of unwanted suitors make a path to my door when I've got things to do."

"How about just…one?" Jethro swallowed past the lump the size of a hay bale lodged in his throat.

There was another heavy sigh from the opposite side of Nutmeg. "One is better than several, but even one could be too many, depending on who it is. Who are you thinking?"

Jethro worried his lip some more. It was far easier leading the mare down the road than to try to lead Susannah in this pivotal conversation. Inhaling so deeply he was afraid his suspenders would snap, Jethro breathed out his response, almost hoping she didn't hear it. "M-me."

Thankfully, Nutmeg's black-maned neck between them prevented Susannah from seeing the strain on his face. Jethro held his breath, expecting any moment to hear her laugh, followed by "Are you kidding?" His response—"*Ja, ja*, I was. Wouldn't that have been funny?"—was on the tip of his tongue.

Instead, it was silent on the other side of the mare. The only sounds were the creaking of the parts of leather harness Nutmeg still wore and the swish of long grass as the odd trio strode through it. When those, along with an occasional buzz of an insect, continued to be the only things his straining ears picked up, Jethro wondered if Susannah had heard him.

He pressed his lips together. He couldn't say it again. He'd barely been able to voice it the first time. It was a foolish idea, made incredibly so by speaking it out loud. His shoulders sagged with dejection. But since he had made a fool of himself, he was glad it was to Susannah. She was the only woman he trusted enough to do so in front of. And even with that, a sweat born of embarrassment dampened his back.

"Why?" Susannah ducked under Nutmeg's neck to appear in front of him. The startled mare wasn't near as stunned as Jethro.

He froze midstride. A quick scan of Susannah's face revealed none of the smirk he'd feared. Nor any incredulity indicating she thought he was demented. If her expression showed anything, it was a bit of concern.

Following a shaky exhale, Jethro struggled to respond. "It would b-be a reprieve for b-both of us? M-my p-parents want m-me t-to start looking for a wife again. I'm…not in a hurry t-to d-do so. B-but it's hard t-to say no t-to them. They d-don't listen t-to no when they d-don't want t-to hear it. At least when they hear it from m-me."

Susannah's mouth opened, like she was going to say something. When she didn't, encouraged, Jethro continued. "So I thought, as you d-don't want a suitor, and I d-don't want t-to b-be one, if I acted like *your* suitor—for appearances only," he hastened to add "—it would t-take care of b-both our p-problems. At least for a while."

Eyes narrowing, Susannah slowly closed her mouth. After considering him for a moment, it tipped into a slanted smile. "Your parents won't like it. You, walking out with me. I'm totally unsuitable for you."

Jethro smiled himself, relaxing for the first time since the ludicrous idea had come to him. "I know. That's p-part of the p-plan's appeal."

She eyed him a moment longer, her hooded gaze transitioning to reveal a hint of mischief in her brown eyes. "What do you propose, on this fake proposal?"

With the hand not holding the reins, Jethro stroked the short beard that proclaimed he'd been married. "I...hadn't gotten that far." He looked back down the road to his parents' small farmstead. "I suppose a start is m-making sure they see us t-together. Or hear about us from others. Which won't t-take m-much d-due t-to the healthy grapevine in the d-district." Casting a guarded glance at Susannah, he tentatively lifted a brow, aware her question didn't mean she was agreeing to his suggestion.

With a sigh, she watched Leroy's buggy top the far hill before shifting her attention to her farmyard just a stone's throw ahead. Reaching out, she ran a gentle hand down the now serene mare's nose.

"Does being a suitor include fixing the buggy?"

"*Nee.* It was a friend that offered t-to fix it and a friend that will." He grinned. "B-but I suppose it's something a suitor would d-do."

Susannah smiled ruefully. "Will the suitor still be a friend when the courtship has run its course? There are a number of men in the district who might come calling as suitors, but only a few who're always welcome to visit as friends. I wouldn't want to lose a long-term friendship for a short-term courtship."

"*Nee.*" Jethro shook his head adamantly. "This one will always b-be a friend first."

She was going to say yes. Jethro didn't stop to consider why the knowledge elated him beyond outmaneuvering his parents. "Even enough to choke d-down your cooking a t-time or t-two." He almost winked at her. Jethro was momentarily stunned at the temptation. He never winked. But the urge to do so felt very good. "M-maybe that's what'll convince folks we're actually walking out. For sure and certain, no one would eat it m-more than once otherwise."

Susannah frowned as she swatted at him. "My cooking isn't that bad. And it's not like I can't cook. It's that there's always something else that needs to be done, so the cooking either gets hurried or forgotten." Giving Nutmeg a last pat, she ducked back under the mare's neck.

"We'll talk about it more tomorrow when you come to fix the buggy. It's been a while since I've had a welcomed suitor. I'm not sure I remember how."

With a soft click of his tongue, Jethro prompted the mare into motion. Some of his exuberance receded. He wasn't sure if he remembered how, either, as it'd been a while since he'd been a suitor as well. And even then, he wasn't sure he'd been a welcomed one. He'd failed at being a suitor for the right reasons. How could he hope to succeed when doing it for the wrong ones?

Chapter Two

She couldn't put it off any longer. Susannah drained the sink and shook the dishwater from her hands. Sucking in a fortifying breath, she looked out the window to where her teenage hired hand's push scooter leaned against the side of the big white barn.

She'd intended to talk with him yesterday, but the young man had already been gone by the time she and Jethro had walked Nutmeg back to the farm. Although her hired hand was late—again—for work today, she'd been relieved he'd arrived after Amos had departed for school and her daughter Rebecca had left for work.

John Schlabach always did what Susannah asked him to do, but there were times when he fixed his eyes on her with an unreadable expression that she felt…uneasy. Anticipating the coming confrontation, she was comforted more than she wanted to admit when Jethro had driven his rig up the lane shortly after the young man's arrival.

After drying her hands, Susannah absently pulled the dish towel back and forth between them. Although comforted by his arrival, she was also relieved that Jethro had gone straight to the damaged buggy he'd deposited by the shed yesterday. She wasn't sure what she'd say yet if he'd come to the house to continue yesterday's odd conversation. She hadn't said yes to his nonproposal, but she hadn't said no, either. As she watched him bend over the damaged buggy shaft, a smile tugged at her.

He looked so different from the quiet, skinny child she'd been a *kinder minder* to years ago. Susannah had felt sorry for Jethro then. Never a patient woman, Ruby Weaver had been particularly short with her older son. She hadn't seemed to know what to do with him and the unexpected cleft lip and palate that'd revealed itself upon his birth. Over the years, Jethro had had a series of community-funded surgeries to correct the split in his lip and roof of his mouth. With each one, Ruby's unhappiness with the boy seemed to grow.

Noting this, Susannah had given Jethro as much positive attention as possible when she'd been with him. She'd discovered his subtle humor, his hardworking, caring character, his eagerness to please. He'd grown into a dependable, respected man in the community. One she was happy to call a friend.

Of course, he was still quiet, even reserved, around most folks. Some of that was probably due to his nature, perhaps more to his stutter. Susannah had been glad yet concerned for Jethro when she'd heard he was marrying his brother's widow. He and the fragile, emotional, Louisa had seemed an odd fit.

Susannah snorted. Now the truly odd fit would be Jethro and herself. Her lips twitched. She'd be surprised if anyone took a courtship between them seriously.

Hanging up the dish towel, her gaze lingered on the man working by the buggy. Except perhaps Jethro. Susannah felt no compunction in disrupting the bishop's plans for her life, at least temporarily, but not if it would negatively affect Jethro. Her gaze grew troubled. What if this solitary, warmhearted man got too attached in the charade? Susannah might not've been courted for a long time, but even she recalled the enjoyment of close companionship. The thrill of a certain someone paying particular attention to you. What if a potentially lonely person mistook that companionship for…something else? She didn't want him to be hurt.

Aren't you getting a bit full of yourself, Susannah? Isn't it hochmut *to think an attractive man in his prime would be interested in you when, if he overcame some shyness, he could probably have his pick of any of the young ladies in the district?*

Now there was another possibility. Maybe a fake courtship would help Jethro overcome some of his reserve. Help him become more confident to go courting in the future, as surely he would. *At least with Jethro, his interest in marriage, even if it's artificial, will be about you and not about the farm. He has his own prosperous place. Unlike some others, he doesn't need or want yours. He, at least, is straightforward in his motives.*

She was going to do it. Susannah shook her head at her foolishness but couldn't suppress the spark of excitement that flared inside her. *Ach,* the community would talk about her, gossip that she was a silly woman, but she didn't mind. It was much better than being set upon by a string of men she had no interest in. And maybe by the time their temporary courtship was over, she'd have time to identify someone who *would* be a reasonable choice—someone with maybe as much interest in her as in her farm—to come calling.

Her excitement popped like one of the soap bubbles she'd used to blow for Jethro as a child when her gaze shifted to the scooter leaning by the barn. In the meantime, she had to deal with her soon-to-be-ex hired hand. Susannah couldn't and wouldn't keep on anyone who'd intentionally hurt one of her animals. And she couldn't dawdle in the house when he might have intentions of harming another of her livestock.

Lifting the lid on a counter canister marked Sugar, she counted out enough bills to cover what she owed the youth. After a brief hesitation, she added a few more before crumpling them in a fisted hand and resolutely heading for the door.

Susannah felt Jethro's eyes on her as she marched across the barnyard. Striving for a confidence she wasn't feeling, she didn't look in his direction, but was well aware of where he knelt by the damaged buggy.

Upon reaching the barn, Susannah paused outside the door. The edge of the wood cut into her palm as she curled a hand over the open Dutch door and peered into the barn's dim interior. Inhaling a shivery breath, she called into its cavernous depths. "John?"

After a moment of stillness, there was a movement in one of the stalls. A young man stepped out of the shadows, his tall, gangly figure seeming not much wider than one of the barn's posts. When he didn't move farther, Susannah called again. "Would you please come here? I need to talk with you."

Although her heart was hammering over what she had to do, it still ached for the youth as he trudged closer. Unhooking the door, Susannah swung it open and stepped back as John approached. Following her lead, he exited into the farmyard. His eyes were unreadable under the shade of his battered flat-brimmed straw hat.

Susannah cleared her throat. "John, there was a nail in Nutmeg's harness collar yesterday. Do you know anything about that?"

The youth didn't speak. Grimacing, he shifted his feet.

"It hurt her so much, we went into the ditch. She could've been injured worse, possibly even broken a leg and had to be put down. I don't think you'd want that. And Amos was with me. He could've been hurt badly."

John was still silent. But he looked away.

"You harnessed her yesterday before we left. I think it would've been something you'd have noticed."

Pressing his lips together, John crossed his arms over his chest.

Stomach twisting with tension, Susannah continued. "Speaking of noticing, I've noticed you haven't been giving *gut* care to the animals. The chicken feed should be almost gone by now. The fact that it isn't, makes me wonder if you're feeding them the amounts you're supposed to. The bedding for the goats isn't nearly as thick as it should be, and it's long past time to be changed. You know what the chores are, John. I could attribute those things to carelessness, or laziness, both of which I'd try to work with you on. But what I can't tolerate is intentionally hurting my animals."

Her soon-to-be-ex hired hand remained studiously silent, his expression rigid.

"Why would you do such a thing, John?" The words were no more than a whisper. Susannah was sincerely troubled and puzzled over his recent behavior.

The young man's shoulders slumped. He toed the gravel at his feet. When he finally lifted his gaze to her, Susannah almost took a step back.

"Are you going to shun me like you did my *daed*?" John's lip was curled in derision, but the effect was spoiled when his voice cracked on the bitter words. His eyes, although hot, also held a flare of fear.

"Your *daed*..." Susannah paused on a heavy sigh. She'd never mentioned Mervin Schlabach in a conversation with his son. But it was one of the reasons—primarily the reason—she'd hired him. She'd felt sorry for the boy. Susannah didn't know how much John knew about why his father had been shunned and ultimately left the community. He would've been very young when it'd happened. Surely the boy was aware...

"I would never do that." She tried a gentle smile to soften the words. "Besides, you know shunning only applies to baptized members of the church. And you haven't been baptized yet. *Nee*, John, I just need to protect my animals. Both in terms of ensuring they're given the care they need to survive and thrive, and that they're protected from harm. I... It makes me sad to tell you I can't trust you on either account. So I have to let you go."

Susannah could tell from his expression that her statement was expected.

He flinched when she swung her hand up. When she opened her fisted fingers to reveal crumpled bills, John stared at them a moment before hesitantly reaching out to pluck them from her palm. Susannah's heart clenched when he carefully flattened them before neatly refolding them to clutch in a grimy hand.

Her throat tight, Susannah nodded toward his scooter. "It might be best if you left now."

John's hard swallow was evident in his gangling neck. He turned toward the scooter, but paused briefly at Susannah's quiet words.

"I still don't understand why, John."

Jerking the scooter's handlebar toward him, he stepped onto the deck with one foot while simultaneously giving a forceful push with the other.

Susannah pressed her hands to her mouth as he careened down the lane and shot onto the blacktop.

I will not cry, she murmured into her fingertips, although she ached for the young man. Tears might threaten, but they'd never be allowed to fall. She watched until John was a speck in the distance.

Exhaling a sigh that seemed to reach down to her bare toes, Susannah lowered her hands. *Now what*? She had a busy farm and not enough labor to work it. Amos helped, but at eleven years old, he was still in school and would be until he finished eighth grade. Had she made the right decision? Would half a hired hand have been better than none? At the quiet jingle of a halter that filtered through the open barn door, Susannah firmed her lips. Not at the risk to her animals. *Ach*, she wasn't afraid of hard work. She was just troubled about determining which tasks could afford to wait.

The sunny autumn day mocked her morose mood. The tasks would just have to wait a moment more. Needing to regain her equilibrium, Susannah headed to one of her favorite places on the farm, her small orchard. The dry grass felt warm under her feet as she meandered along the avenue between the Fuji and Braeburn apple trees. Summoning a crooked smile, Susannah tried to absorb the peacefulness of the orchard instead of seeing the fruit-laden trees as more work to be done in the next few weeks. Without help.

An occasional leaf drifted by, gliding on the soft breeze. Reaching to a nearby low branch, Susannah plucked an apple as her mind churned over her options. Rebecca worked at the restaurant in town. If she had a later shift, she could help before work as it would be too dark after. Her married daughter, Rachel, might be willing to lend a hand, but with recent twins who'd made Susannah a *grossmammi*, she had enough on her plate. Perhaps Rachel could spare Miriam Schrock, the hired girl staying with them to help tend the *boppeli*, for a day.

Susannah absently brushed a hand against the faint buzzing at her ear. The serenity of the orchard ended abruptly with a sharp sting on her ankle. Automatically swatting at it, Susannah hissed at instant pain on her other foot. When she glanced down, her breath hitched at the sight of wasps swarming around her legs.

She'd unknowingly walked over a ground nest of yellow jackets.

Flinching at the stings while swatting and slapping at her legs, Susannah was rooted with distress for a moment before realizing a retreat was her best option. Snatching up the hem of her dress, she raced toward the house, frantically flapping her skirt to get the wasps out of it as she ran.

Susannah dashed up the steps to the porch, shaking her skirt to discourage any remaining insects. She didn't feel any new stings, but so many places on her legs were already throbbing, it was hard to tell. Panting, she pressed her skirt out of the way against her legs to peer down at her feet.

Welts were already rising on her ankles and lower legs. From the resonating pain, she knew some of the numerous stings were as high as her knees.

At the touch on her elbow, Susannah jumped and spun, almost stumbling down the steps in her agitation. Jethro's firm but gentle grip instantly tightened, preventing her tumble.

His gaze was sharp under furrowed brows. "Are you all right?"

"I'm not sure. I walked over a yellow jacket nest. They didn't take kindly to trespassers." Susannah tried not to wince at the pulsing pain.

Jethro instantly squatted to examine her lower legs. "Are you allergic?" His tone was as intense as his blue eyes when they shot to hers.

"I hope not. As I've made a poor choice to be a beekeeper if I am." Even as she joked about it, Susannah forced a swallow, ensuring she still had the ability to do so.

Jethro wasn't laughing. If anything, his gaze was more stern. "Have you ever b-been stung this many t-times?"

Susannah didn't think so. In fact, as places on her legs continued to throb, she knew so. She'd had a sting here and there, but never like this. Aware that allergic reactions could get worse with each sting, she touched a hand to her throat. Just because she hadn't been deathly allergic yet didn't mean she never would be.

She didn't resist when Jethro opened the door to the kitchen then gently took her hand and led her inside. "Let's get some b-baking soda and water on those stings."

Susannah had used the remedy before. She didn't look forward to the mixture drying and crumbling off all over the house, but the thought of some relief prompted her to quickly point out the cupboard where she kept her baking ingredients.

Upon ushering her to a kitchen table, Jethro pulled out a chair and helped her settle into it. "B-bowl?" He retrieved one from the cupboard she indicated. Dumping baking soda into it, Jethro crossed to the sink where he dribbled water into it as well. Stirring the mixture with his finger, he returned to where Susannah, fighting a grimace, watched.

Setting the bowl, along with his hat, on the table, Jethro slid out another chair. Susannah frowned as he knelt beside her. When he gingerly touched her ankle, she jumped like she'd been stung again and jerked it away.

"I can do it!" The pain was momentarily forgotten at the startling sensation of his hand on her leg.

"I d-don't know if we're courting yet, b-but I suspect we're going to have our first argument." Ignoring her, Jethro lifted her foot to rest it on the seat of the facing chair. Capturing her other foot, he placed it alongside the first before he calmly reached for the bowl on the table. He regarded Susannah with a raised eyebrow. "*Ja?* Can you see t-the ones on t-the b-back of your legs, t-too?"

Their eyes collided for a moment before she relented with a frown. "*Ach, nee.* But I'll take care of the ones above the hem of my skirt." A hem that fortunately hung down well over her knees.

Nodding, Jethro dipped a finger into the bowl. It was coated with a white paste when he withdrew it.

Susannah tried not to sigh in relief at the cool comfort when he began dabbing the mixture onto her stings. Even so, he must've sensed her tension.

"I know these are hurting." He covered a few more rising welts with the white mixture. Susannah hissed in a breath as he removed a tiny barb, lost by one of the wasps, out of a welt before treating it. Jethro winced in sympathy. "It's strange t-to t-tend t-to your wounds. B-but only fair, I guess, as you'd t-tended t-to m-many of m-mine when I was young."

Susannah suspected he was just talking to distract her. She appreciated his efforts. She wanted to respond in kind. But she couldn't. Because his tending her wounds wasn't the only thing that was strange.

There was also her unexpected reaction. Susannah's breathing shallowed. Heat seeped through her, flushing her skin. Was she allergic after all?

Chapter Three

It only took a moment to determine it wasn't an allergy that was making her senses hum. This hum didn't generate from wasps or their stings. No, this was much, much worse. Her senses were humming from Jethro's soft touch.

Susannah inhaled sharply. Jethro paused in his ministrations to give her another sympathetic glance, probably assuming her distress was because she hurt. *Hopefully* assuming it was because she hurt. Because he must never know what she was feeling. For what she was feeling was ludicrous.

This was Jethro; his folks had been her neighbors since she couldn't remember when. He was at least a decade younger than she was. She'd changed his diapers when he was a *boppeli*.

Unexpectedly dry-mouthed, Susannah watched

Jethro's callused but careful hands as they delicately treated her stings. He shifted, his white shirt stretching over lean but broad shoulders.

He wasn't a *boppeli* any more.

The kitchen was suddenly too quiet. Susannah filled the uncomfortable void with nervous chatter. "I don't know. Two days in a row? I seem to have started a habit of having you tend to me."

Susannah wanted to snatch the words back. She certainly didn't want to draw attention to him taking care of her.

Jethro turned his head to glance at her, the corner of his mouth tipped in a smile. It was a neighborly look. A simple I've-known-you-all-my-life look. But when their gazes caught, they tangled. They lingered. In his eyes, the warmth shared with the tilted smile flared into something else. Awareness? Interest?

Susannah's breath caught at the sight. Oh dear! She worried about him getting too attached. What if she was the one who got the foolish notion this charade was more than what it was? That would embarrass him. And her.

Abruptly, she swept her feet off the chair. They landed with a thump on the floor, jarring the already hard, aching, itchy welts. Gritting her teeth, Susannah sat forward and extended a hand for the bowl. "*Denki*, but I can get the rest."

Jethro sat back on his heels before nodding and handing her the bowl. Pushing to his feet, he turned his back and faced her simple white-painted cupboards.

"Go ahead and t-take care of them. I won't watch."

He may not be watching, but Jethro had always been a good listener. It was quiet for several seconds before the scrape of a chair sliding back and the rustle of material told him she was treating the remaining stings as he'd suggested. He stared at the metal handles on the cupboards as, one by one, he touched his thumbs to where he could feel his pulse beating at the tips of his fingers. *Now wasn't that interesting.*

Although he had hopes, he still wasn't sure what her answer to yesterday's question would be. Would the unexpected surge in his pulse at the look they'd shared cause a problem in that awkward proposal? Crossing his arms over his chest, Jethro pressed hands under his arms until all he felt against his fingertips was the cotton of his shirt. *It couldn't. It wouldn't.* He'd assured her the endeavor wouldn't affect their friendship. It would surely embarrass and dismay Susannah if he were to…what? Fall in love with her?

His face flaming at the prospect, Jethro's attuned ears picked up the quiet tread of bare feet on linoleum and the sound of the bowl being set on the counter. For numerous heartbeats, Susannah didn't move from the counter.

Clearing his throat, he offered over his shoulder, "I've heard that honey works as well."

"At least that's something I have plenty of. And it will stay on much better than this when it dries. You can turn around now."

Jethro pivoted to face her. Susannah stood by the sink, her arms crossed over her chest as well. As he regarded her, a faint blush crept up her cheeks. She hugged her arms more tightly. Jethro's lips almost twitched at the sight they must make, both of them coiled up like a roll of wire fencing. It didn't seem the time to ask about her decision, but he wanted to know, now more than ever, what might be their path forward. Maybe, as his heart finally settled back to normal, it would be better if she said no.

Although they felt as stiff as the Tinman without oil, Jethro lowered his arms. "D-did you think about what I said yesterday?"

Her cheeks still pink, Susannah nodded her

head slowly. *"Ja.* I can see some of the merits of the idea."

"And?"

"Does this count as courting?"

Jethro's pulse kicked up again. "It's an abnormal start."

Susannah smiled faintly. "I suppose that's fitting, as it's an abnormal courtship. What do we do next?"

"I'm not sure." His marrying Louisa had been more of a foregone conclusion than a courtship. Since then, other than a few awkward meals with a young woman his folks had pushed upon him—one who'd fortunately been interested in another man—Jethro had been able to avoid courtship.

Susannah shifted her weight to rub one foot against the paste-marked spots of the other. Bits of powder flaked to the linoleum floor. "Usually the intent of a courting couple is to keep their relationship unknown until it's announced in church, at least for youth in their *rumspringa.*"

Rumspringa—the years when Amish youth were allowed to explore more of the world to determine their decision regarding baptism into the church and to choose a mate—had held no interest for Jethro. Intending to do the former and having no intention of doing the latter, his runaround time had been very short. He'd attended baptism classes as soon as he'd been allowed.

"Our objective would b-be the opposite. We want p-people t-to know. We want m-my folks t-to, at least."

Susannah dropped her arms to her sides. "I suppose, then, we need to be seen together when we wouldn't normally have a reason to be with each other, at least by your folks. That shouldn't be too hard, as they're the next farm down the road."

"B-being here to fix your b-buggy is a start. B-but I should have it d-done b-by the end of the d-day."

"*Denki*, Jethro. I appreciate your help, but I'm sorry to have kept you from your own work."

"It's not a p-problem." Crossing to the table, Jethro picked up his flat-brimmed straw hat. "Speaking of help, it looked like your hired hand went d-down the road. Is he coming b-back?"

Susannah sighed and shook her head. "*Nee*, I had to let him go after what he'd done to Nutmeg."

His gaze sharpened. He couldn't imagine purposely hurting an animal. "So it was intentional?"

It was obvious Susannah shared his sentiment. "He didn't say, but *ja,* I suspect so."

"Why?"

"That, I don't know."

"It leaves you short-handed at a b-busy time."

Susannah sagged against the counter. "*Ja.* I fear so."

"What needs t-to be d-done t-today?"

"What doesn't? I need to check on Nutmeg. I'm not sure if John cleaned the horse stalls, or the goat pen. After that, there's the garden and some remaining field work…" Her voice trailed off.

Glancing at the white residue in the bowl on the counter, Susannah shook her head wearily. "And now, the yellow jacket nest. It's too close to my beehives for comfort. If the wasps have any kind of food shortage, they'll attack my hives. If it's a big nest, they'll kill my bees and take the honey. I can reduce the entrances into the hive so the bees have a better chance of defending it. Though yellow jackets do serve some purpose in nature, to protect my bees—" her lips thinned in a humorless smile "—I'd prefer to take out the nest." She grimaced. "If I can find it."

Jethro's gaze dropped to the red welts marring the slender legs below her hemline. He'd been stung by wasps before. Some stings could feel like a baseball bat had made a solid connection. She had to be in pain. And itchy. Whether friend or suitor, he couldn't let her risk getting stung again. "I'll t-take care of the livestock when I finish with the b-buggy."

Susannah instantly straightened from her slump. "I couldn't ask you to do that."

"You d-didn't ask. I offered. What you need t-to d-do is get off your feet and continue t-to t-take care of those stings. I counted at least seven, p-plus whatever you've t-treated."

Jethro could read from her expression that she wouldn't mind doing as he'd suggested. But wouldn't. At least not yet. She'd always been a stubborn female. "Susannah, m-most of m-my crops are already in for the year. I have a b-bit of t-time t-to spare t-to help." He gave her a half smile. "It's what friends, if not suitors, d-do. P-plus, it gives m-my folks m-more of a chance t-to see m-me here," he reminded her.

Susannah regarded him with lowered brow before finally conceding with a sigh, "I could use any help you can provide."

He nodded. Having been pushed frequently in his life, he knew when not to. "How d-do you p-plan t-to find the nest?"

Wincing, she bent to scratch at the red welts on her legs. More powder drifted to the linoleum floor. "I need to catch a wasp, mark it and follow it back to the nest and mark the nest when I find it. Later this evening, when all the wasps are inside, I'll pour soapy water...or—" Opening the cupboard from where he'd gotten the baking soda behind her, she shifted a few jars around. "Molasses. I should have enough of that to seal the nest. The wasps get trapped in the thickness."

Jethro eyed her dubiously. "How d-do you p-plan to catch a wasp and m-mark it?"

Susannah glanced over her shoulder with a wry smile. "Carefully. With gloves, a lidded cup and this." She withdrew a bag of powdered sugar from the cupboard.

Jethro raised his eyebrow. He wasn't going to ask. "Find a b-big p-pair of gloves. I'll catch the wasp."

She opened her mouth like she was going to argue. Closing it again, she bit her lip and rubbed one leg against the other again. There was now more powder on the floor than her legs. "I won't argue with that today."

"Why d-don't you sit for a m-moment with ice or something while I t-take care of the live-stock? Then we'll catch a wasp."

An Amish woman rarely had time to sit during the day. Even under the circumstances, he didn't think Susannah would make an ex-

ception. Surprisingly, she nodded. She must
be in considerable pain, indeed. Pulling out
a drawer, she retrieved a plastic bag before
hobbling to the gas-powered refrigerator and
withdrawing a handful of ice from the freezer
section to drop it into the bag.

"You m-might also t-try a sweet p-pickle
juice compress. The alum in it is supposed
t-to help." With that suggestion, Jethro headed
out the door.

Two hours later, he and Susannah were
standing in the shade of one of her apple trees.
Jethro's shirt sleeves were rolled down. On
his hands was a worn leather pair of gloves.
Susannah attention flicked around their surrounding area, searching for potential captives
for the cup she held, its bottom covered with
a powdery white substance.

Her distraction gave him a chance to study
her profile. Her features were relaxed, but the
strain of the day's pain was evident in her
tanned face. The only hint to her years was
the creases at the corners of her eyes. Ones
that crinkled when she smiled. He remembered her as always smiling when he was
young. But with running a farm while nurs-
ing an ill husband before losing him around a
year ago, and taking care of her family alone

since, she hadn't had a lot to smile about. Neither of them had.

Susannah had had a nice smile. It surprised Jethro how much he wanted to put another one on her face.

"I can understand how you got your reputation, or lack of it, for b-baking skills. You d-don't use your groceries for cooking b-but for farm work. M-molasses and sugar for wasps. B-baking soda for your legs. I think I'll stay and see what you feed the goats t-tonight."

As Jethro intended, her lips curved at his teasing. The tenseness in her shoulders eased fractionally. He found himself relaxing as well.

He'd only been six when a teenage Susannah had married Vernon Mast. The rumored reason had been to save her family's farm after her father had died. Jethro hadn't been and still wasn't one for rumors, but his *mamm* was. Six was a young age to listen and remember conversation, but Susannah had minded him frequently when his *mamm* wasn't able, and he'd liked her. She'd been…fun, a rarity in his life back then. She had never stared at his scar, which'd been much more prominent. Perhaps what'd struck him the most was that she'd always been patient while he'd struggled to communicate. That was probably why he spoke more easily with her than any other woman.

Whatever the reason, Jethro had wondered when she hadn't come around anymore. His *mamm* had shushed him when he'd asked about her absence and told him Susannah had her own family to attend to now. As had Jethro's *mamm*, since his little *bruder* had soon appeared. His perfect little *bruder*. Jethro stared unseeing at the ripe apple in front of him as his shoulders rose over a deep sigh.

"It's not as bad as rumors claim. As the youngest *dochder*, by the time I arrived, my folks had given up on having a *sohn*. So while my older *schweschdere* mostly stayed inside and helped my *mamm*, I was outside working with my *daed*." Susannah's gaze shifted to the collection of white buildings down the little rise. "It's not that I can't cook or bake. It's just that I'd still rather be outside, and frequently am. So sometimes food is a little too done or…"

"Not d-done enough? Or b-both at once?"

She scowled as she idly shook the powdered sugar inside the container. "You heard about that?" She peered at him. "Of course you did. I'm sure everyone has. Still, it had a benefit."

Jethro raised an eyebrow.

"Now I'm only asked to provide bread and church spread on Sundays and other gatherings." Her eyes crinkled as they joined her grin. "It cuts down on what I have to prepare. Especially when Rebecca makes the bread."

They both froze at a nearby buzzing sound. Susannah flinched when a striped yellow jacket flew idly over her shoulder to land on a small branch nearby. As it worked its way to a dangling apple, Jethro carefully took the cup from her. Removing the lid, he cautiously raised it above the distracted wasp with the cup below. When the wasp lifted off the branch, Jethro slammed down the lid, knocking the yellow jacket into the cup. Quickly securing the lid, he rocked the now vibrating container to and fro, coating the startled wasp with the white powder.

"Now what?"

"Now we let him out to betray his community."

His lips quirked. "You're vindictive for an Amish p-person. What happened t-to t-turn the other ankle?"

"Both ankles have turned hot. And aching. And itchy." Susannah looked up at him with an impish expression. "The wasps are hungry. I'm planning on sharing the contents of my cupboard with them. It's a neighborly thing to do. What more could they want?"

Gazing down into her face, Jethro's fingers tightened on the container. He knew he needed to be careful about what he wanted in this courtship he'd suggested. It was to be an act. Something to fool his parents. It wouldn't do if the only thing that ended up foolish about their ploy was him actually falling for Susannah.

Hours later, Susannah headed for the orchard, a heavy jar of molasses in her hand. The time had fled since they'd released the wasp and watched it zigzag a path before settling in the grass to disappear from view. Creeping closer, Jethro had identified the hole in the ground and carefully stuck a stick trailing a bit of white fabric at the entrance.

Her heartrate accelerated as she climbed the hill in the tranquil moonlit night. Not because of the uncertain task ahead, but because of the man at her side.

Jethro had gone into town to obtain a part for the wrecked buggy, teasing Susannah that he'd get lunch while he was there. She'd countered that she didn't mind, it saved her from stopping to fix something on the farm. She'd kept busy—as always—while he was gone. But what was new was the breathless lift to her heart when his rig had driven up her lane later in the afternoon.

Upon finishing the buggy repair, Jethro had

joined her in the garden, harvesting the last of the squash and pumpkins, and pulling the vines to prepare the patch for tilling in fertilizer. Amos had returned from school by the time they'd finished. Her son had assisted Jethro in doing chores while she'd gone inside to prepare supper. And took her time doing so to ensure it was one of her better meals. When Jethro hesitantly took a bite after she'd invited him to stay once they'd finished chores, he'd met her watchful gaze and raised his eyebrows in appreciation. And lifted Susannah's heart further.

Saying he couldn't let her face the nest alone in case the wasps rallied for an attack—and besides, his rig needed to be parked in her yard just in case someone should drive by— Jethro had stayed until darkness had settled and the full moon had risen. He'd listened quietly while Amos told of the softball game at recess and Rebecca had shared news of the potential sale of the restaurant in town.

The evening had been…nice. Too nice. It touched on an ache that was far different from the residual stings throbbing around Susannah's ankles.

Don't get used to it. This is only temporary. Jethro is a man in his prime. He has a successful farm of his own. He doesn't need to marry an old widow to get one. Tucking the jar against her side, Susannah crossed her arms over her chest.

"Cold?" Jethro murmured. The autumn's evening temperature had dropped as quickly as the earlier setting sun.

"Nee." She nodded toward the stake with its pale streaming material. "Just hope this works."

A barred owl in the surrounding dark fringe of woods called its iconic cry. *Whocooksfo-ryou?* Before they'd gone a few more steps, another owl answered from farther in the distance. *Whocooksforyouall?*

Jethro bumped his shoulder against hers. "I know who d-doesn't."

Susannah's heart squeezed at the action. *Don't get any ideas. It doesn't mean anything. The man is just practicing before we take this courting act public.* But from the way her pulse skittered, she didn't think Jethro needed any practice. "Provoke me all you want, I'm still not giving up the jar."

They'd had a quiet yet intense debate over who would crouch by the nest and pour the molasses. Jethro didn't want Susannah to risk getting stung again. Susannah silently figured the stings might do her some good at the present. Get her mind off the moonlit night and the unexpected attractiveness of the man beside her, and remind her that Jethro was there for a purpose. And it was because he *wasn't* looking for a wife, not because he was.

Unscrewing the jar's lid, she crept up to the stake. Absent of artificial light, as any light would attract the wasps, it took a moment of searching to find the hole in the tall grass. When she knelt and poured the molasses down it, she flinched at the initial buzzing. But as more thick brown substance flowed into the hole, the sound was increasingly muffled. She tipped the jar upside down for a moment to prompt the sluggish material to drain out. Recapping the lid, she stood and stepped back.

Jethro relieved her of the now empty jar. "There. Your b-bees are safe."

Susannah nodded, hoping that was the case. She'd check tomorrow.

"I've never heard of a female Amish b-beekeeper," Jethro observed as they started back down the hill to where her white barn and house gleamed in the reflected moonlight.

Susannah smiled softly at memories. "My *daed* kept them. As he had no sons, I'd take care of the hives with him. When he was gone, I just didn't want to look up on the hill and not see them there anymore. So I kept a few of them."

Jethro nodded as he walked silently beside her. His steps slowed as he looked up until he drifted to a halt.

Susannah presumed he was gazing at the stars. She stopped, tipping her head back, as well, to take in the magnificent display. With the clear night, along with the absence of ground lights in the Amish neighborhood, the overhead glow seemed to press so close you could almost reach up to touch it.

"And something I've never d-done is walk in the m-moonlight with a woman. It's nice." His gaze remained on the stars, but Susannah heard his quiet murmur in the stillness of the evening.

She had to lower her head so she could swallow past the sudden dryness in her mouth. "You don't have to say that. There's no one to hear or see us."

When he looked at her, she could easily make out his crooked smile. "P-perhaps. But m-my *m-mamm* has sharp eyes, sharp ears and a nosy nature. And her kitchen window faces this way."

Susannah turned to squint at the farmhouse across the field. All she could make out was a very faint glow from inside the house, most likely from a gas light or lantern. "If she is, she's not seeing much."

"We can fix that." He extended his hand to her.

For an instant, Susannah stared blankly at his work-roughened palm. She'd never walked in the moonlight with a man, other than with her late husband while looking for escaped livestock. And she'd never held hands with one, just for connection's sake. Not even her husband. Her breathing shallowed. Remembering Jethro's jolting touch earlier today, she tangled her fingers into her apron. "If we jump into it too fast, they might suspect it's not a real courtship."

Crossing her arms over her chest, Susannah began walking again. "It has gotten considerably chillier, hasn't it?" She hoped he wouldn't be upset, but her senses were already foolishly affected by the surprising pleasantness of the earlier evening with Jethro and her family and the current alluring surroundings. It wouldn't do to agitate them further.

She blew out a quiet breath in relief when Jethro fell into step beside her, seemingly unoffended. Side by side, they ambled down to the farmyard to where he'd already harnessed his Standardbred as they'd waited for full darkness. Jethro climbed into the buggy. "T-tomorrow," was all he said before directing his horse down the lane.

Watching the rig depart, Susannah absently rubbed her hands together before reaching down to scratch at her ankles. She frowned with concern. Not for her itchy and achy skin, but her heart, which was acting in a similar manner.

Be careful, Susannah. He's not for you. He's young. He needs someone who can give him a family. And that's not you. Remedies involving baking soda and pickle juice won't do anything to heal a broken heart.

Chapter Four

Susannah wiped down the countertop, her movements brisk with agitation. She had so much she needed to be doing today instead of playing hostess to an unwanted suitor. But Bishop Weaver had been adamant when he'd cornered her after church last Sunday.

It'd been a year since Vernon had died. It was time for her to remarry. The farm was too big for her to run alone. His admonishing recitations were like the order of hymns in their church service; he'd been voicing the same ones to her every church Sunday in the same sequence.

Striding to the table, Susannah scrubbed furiously at a spot of honey dripped by Amos at breakfast. She was accustomed to running the farm by herself, even with a husband. Both while Vernon had been sick and before, when he'd found things he'd rather do than work the farm that Susannah had inherited as the youngest girl in a family of daughters. *Ja*, it was difficult, particularly without a hired hand. But now with Jethro's help...

She paused while swiping the dishrag over the rest of the oak table. *With Jethro's help.* His help made a big difference. Both on the farm and as a pretend beau, which would hopefully make this the last visit of an unwanted suitor, at least for a while.

As far as a wanted one...her gaze drifted to where Jethro had parked his buggy by the barn when he'd arrived a short while ago. She'd had a lot of time *not* sleeping last night after their moonlit walk to think about that. *Ja,* she'd had flickers of awareness that Jethro was no longer a *boppeli* or little boy. And she was no longer an immature girl. Nor was she married anymore. And neither was he.

They were both single adults.

The flickers had been...preposterous. And that's how she needed to treat them. Even if no one saw through their sham, the community knew they were totally unsuitable for each other. As did she. So any wayward flickers would just have to be extinguished. She could do that. She was well acquainted with stifling longings over the years and being satisfied with what she had.

Crossing to the sink, Susannah dropped the dishrag into soapy water with a splash. She supposed she should provide some refreshments for the pending visit, although she didn't want to encourage the unwanted guest. The goats had taken longer than expected this morning. She usually enjoyed her time with them but they'd put her behind today and left her little time to get ready.

Shooting a glance at the clock, she realized her potential suitor was to arrive in fifteen minutes. Susannah froze at the *clip-clop* of hooves coming up the lane that drifted through the open window. The only thing she liked less than a courting widower was an overeager one.

With a waist-deep sigh, she brushed a quick hand down her apron and headed to the kitchen door in time to see Leroy Albrecht descend from his buggy. Although she'd known his deceased wife, they hadn't been close friends. Still, Susannah had a great deal of admiration for the departed Mrs. Albrecht. Anyone who could live with Leroy had more patience than Susannah could ever summon. She'd rather spend the day with the goats. While she watched, her assigned suitor rubbed his hands together as he glanced around her well-kept farm with an assessing expression. *Ja*, she'd definitely rather spend it with the goats. She held the door open for him with a gritted-teeth smile and a false welcome.

Without pausing to respond to her greeting, Leroy made his way to the oak table, slid out a chair and settled into it. The last place Susannah wanted to be was sitting across from his florid face. Flicking on the gas oven, she pulled a mixing bowl from the cupboard.

"I thought I'd mix up some cookies."

Leroy nodded in agreement. "I'd sure appreciate that. My wife, Arleta, was *wunderbar* in the kitchen. It's essential my next one is as well. I'd heard about your cooking, so when the bishop mentioned I should pay you a call, I was apprehensive. But I thought, for sure and certain, she can't be as bad as they say."

In the process of beating the butter and sugar in the bowl, Susannah paused an instant before her wooden spoon whipped a little faster. *Oh I can't, can I?*

"I don't think there's much more important work for a woman to do than to take care of her man. 'Course it's well known that you've always been a hard worker on the farm and that's important, too."

Ja, Susannah decided. *I can.* Jerking the baking soda down from the cupboard, she jiggled the box to determine the quantity inside. Leroy's wife had needed to be a hard worker. Because he certainly wasn't. Retrieving her measuring cups, Susannah poured a heaping amount of baking soda into the quarter cup measurer and dumped it into the batter.

"That's why I've been seeking out the more—" Susannah could feel the man's eyes on her as he hesitated "—mature widows."

Susannah wasn't feeling very mature as she added three times the amount of salt the recipe stated before eyeballing an amount of flour and spices and beating the batter more vigorously than any electric mixer could. The man couldn't see what she was doing anyway with her more…mature figure in the way.

Snagging a cookie sheet from a lower cupboard, Susannah banged it on the counter to drown out whatever he was droning on about how his late wife cooked and baked so wonderfully. After spooning the dough onto the sheet, she popped it into the oven and turned to face her unwanted guest.

"My wife was a *gut* housekeeper." Leroy shifted to gaze around the rest of what he could see of her home from the kitchen. Susannah watched his eyes linger on the two baskets of laundry she'd pulled from the clothesline last evening and hadn't yet had time to put away. Leroy grimaced at the evidence that she might not be up to his standards, but his expression when he turned back to Susannah indicated he'd overlook the fact if necessary.

A flush unrelated to her vigor in stirring the batter climbed up Susannah's neck.

"It sure was a dry drive over. If you wouldn't mind getting me a drink?"

"*Nee. Nee,* I wouldn't mind at all." Reaching for a pitcher, Susannah fixed a drink that would be a fitting companion for the upcoming cookies.

It wasn't a surprise when a short time later Leroy decided she wouldn't be much of a match for him. Susannah was still smiling at the expression on his face when, after dubiously considering the flat blob of cookie on his plate, he bit into it. When he took a drink, her unwelcomed suitor's eyes bulged and his face reddened to a degree that she wondered for a moment if she'd have to hurry down to the phone shack to call in Gabe Bartel, the community's local EMS.

Fortunately, Leroy recovered quickly, shoving away from the table so forcefully the glass of lemonade tipped over. With a wary glance in her direction, he headed for the door.

"*Mach's gut.*" Susannah called a cheery farewell as it slammed behind him. With a satisfied smile, she grabbed a dishcloth to clean up the mess.

The first thing Jethro noticed when Susannah responded to his knock on her door with a greeting to enter was a pitcher of what looked like lemonade on the table, along with some curious-looking cookies. In a hurry to get his chores done to help at her place, he'd left his farm without eating breakfast and only gulping down a hasty cup of coffee.

Hoping she wouldn't mind, he grabbed a glass from the drainer, strode to the table and poured it full of lemonade.

"Don't drink that," Susannah directed without turning around from where she worked at the sink.

Jethro paused with the glass halfway to his lips.

Turning to face him, she reached for it. "It isn't for you. You won't like it."

Jethro eyed the pale yellow liquid in the glass. It looked like perfectly good lemonade to him. After cleaning out the barn, he could almost taste its tartness cutting through the dust that seemed to coat his mouth. Pushing back the brim of his hat with his opposing wrist, he rubbed it across his sweaty forehead.

"You d-don't share lemonade at your house?"

"Not when I make it to chase away potential suitors." Susannah's lips twitched as her hand dropped and she propped it on her hip. "Go ahead. Try it. Let me know if I was successful."

Now eyeing the glass suspiciously, Jethro cautiously took a sip. At the first taste, he scrunched his eyes closed and puckered his mouth. Upon recovering, he set the glass on the table and nudged it farther away with a forefinger. When he glanced at Susannah, she was watching, the smile in her brown eyes matched by the one on her lips.

"D-did it work?"

She wrinkled her nose. "I hope so. He left fast enough. A bit of vinegar in the lemonade helped. But time will tell. Don't eat the cookies, either."

It seemed a shame. They were cooling on the rack on the table. Although haphazard in size and shape, hungry as he was, they still looked tempting.

"Probably enough baking soda in there to use them as a salt lick." Susannah pursed her lips. "I don't like to waste things, but I hesitate to even feed them to the goats. Contrary to myth, goats don't really eat everything. They're pretty good about avoiding things that aren't good for them. Which would include these cookies."

"The visit needed such d-drastic m-measures?"

Susannah poured his glass into the sink, rinsed it and refilled it from a pitcher of tea in the refrigerator. "Some people can't take a subtle hint. Or they're determined. But not as determined as I am in not wanting to marry that particular person."

From the barn, Jethro had watched Leroy Albrecht drive his rig up the lane. He'd smiled when the man had hitched up his trousers and strode confidently to the house. Jethro hadn't been able to see Susannah's expression when she'd met her visitor at the door, but recalling her reaction to the man yesterday, he'd been tempted to watch the show and finish the barn work later. But he liked his own privacy and extended it to others accordingly. Still, it would've been amusing. He knew Leroy well enough to be aware of the man's appetite. The cookies must be bad, indeed, if they were able to drive him off.

As he eyed the cookies, his stomach growled. Loud enough for Susannah to hear as she frowned. "Are you hungry?"

Jethro scratched his beard. "P-probably not enough t-to t-try those."

Susannah nodded with wry acknowledgment as she opened a cupboard door. "I think I have other options. Hmm, there's some cookies from the Bent N' Dent, or there's bread and church spread."

As a busy widower, Jethro was well familiar with food from the local store that sold damaged package and expired goods. Opportunities for homemade bread and the popular peanut butter, marshmallow crème Amish mixture came less frequently. And as far as he knew from Sunday meals, both the offerings were safe. "Church spread sounds *gut*."

Taking his glass of tea to the table, Jethro sat as Susannah efficiently cut a few thick slices of bread and set them, a butter knife and a jar of spread in front of him.

He sighed as he slathered some of the creamy mixture onto a slice. "I think the b-buggy is fixed. B-but I t-took a look at the harness t-today. I need t-to get some things t-to repair the p-places I had t-to cut t-to free the m-mare when she was d-down. Should've remembered them yesterday." He been too distracted thinking of their recent arrangement, but he wasn't going to admit that. "I need t-to go b-back t-to Miller's Creek t-today so you have a harness when you need it." Taking a bite, he eyed her thoughtfully. "Want t-to go with m-me?"

He'd anticipated the words before she hastened to say them. "I don't have time."

Finishing the rest of that piece, he nodded understandably as he chewed. "T-true. B-but d-do you have t-time to m-make another b-batch of goat-rejected cookies for an unwanted visitor?"

Susannah scowled at him. "The goats didn't reject my cookies. I refuse to feed the cookies to them. And what does that have to do with a trip to town?"

Jethro picked up the second slice of bread. "It'd b-be a chance for folks t-to see us t-together. Get word out of our...relationship. M-might stop some future visits," he said, tipping his head toward the cookies. "B-besides, I figured you m-might need some groceries, the way you use up yours on first-aid, wasp slaying and wasted cookies."

Sinking into a chair across the table from him, Susannah narrowed her eyes in a mock glare. Jethro concentrated on smearing the second slice with church spread to keep his lips from twitching.

She huffed out a breath. "I suppose there's merit in that."

Jethro lifted the bread to his mouth to hide his smile. "Out of curiosity, who are m-my... competitors? Who else would m-my *d-daed* b-be sending your way?" Although he was familiar and, to his knowledge, on good terms with everyone in the district, Jethro minded his own business and didn't pay attention to the social undercurrents of the community. He knew the men who weren't married, but not those who might want to be.

Susannah fiddled with a cookie on the cooling rack. "There's a few I've caught casting occasional unexpected glances my way recently." When Jethro didn't say anything, just raised an eyebrow, she continued, although with obvious reluctance. "It seems like Henry Troyer is ready to marry again. I think after the... challenges that Lydia gave him, he wants some help with the rest of the *kinder* at home."

Jethro nodded. Henry was a *gut* man who'd lost his wife a few years ago. Jethro might not pay much attention, but even he'd noticed that one of Henry's older daughters, Lydia, had been more than a little fast. He hadn't been too surprised when he'd heard she'd gone to live with relatives in Pennsylvania.

"Thomas Riehl's children have moved to Indiana to work in the factories where they build recreational vehicles. I would imagine he's lonely." She furrowed her forehead. "And I suppose David Neuenschwander."

Jethro raised his eyebrows at the name. "D-David? He's an old b-boy."

"Just because he never married, doesn't mean he doesn't want to."

Heat crept up Jethro's neck at her gentle chiding. If he hadn't married Louisa at his parents' urging, and her reluctant acceptance, he'd probably be an old boy—the Amish term for an older bachelor—too. "Well, I know he's *gut* with horses. I heard that when Samuel Schrock gets a really skittish one from the t-track, he leaves them with D-David for a b-bit t-to work with them b-before he b-brings them home." And if Samuel, the local horse trader, who was an excellent horseman himself, trusted David, the man must really have a gentle touch with the animals.

Susannah wrinkled her nose. "I don't mean to imply that they're not *gut* men. They are. I just don't have time or interest right now in trying to determine which might be a *gut* man for me and my family. And for the farm."

Brushing the crumbs from his fingers, Jethro stood from the table. "I guess that m-means we go into t-town t-today t-together and let them think you've p-picked m-me."

* * *

Susannah's gaze trailed after Jethro as he headed out the door to ready his buggy for the trip. Her fingers tapped on the table as she considered the men she'd mentioned, all the men in the district for that matter. Jethro was indeed a good pick. Her lips slanted in a rueful smile as she rose from the chair.

But while he might be a *gut* man for her, Susannah knew she wasn't the right wife for him.

Chapter Five

Susannah's pulse surged as Jethro settled onto the buggy seat next to her. It felt odd to be sitting on the left side—the wife's side—of a seat again. She twisted her hands in her lap. Did she really want to be doing this? Agreeing to Jethro's plan when they were isolated on the farm was one thing. But actually taking it public in their community? She smoothed out her apron before resting her damp palms on it.

Certainly, it might give her some peace from the unwanted visits of men the bishop directed her way. But at what cost? She normally wasn't one who worried about what people thought of her, but—sneaking a glance at Jethro's strong, solid profile—would they laugh at a foolish older woman for encouraging a courtship from a man more than ten years her junior? One who could, and should, be seeking a spouse closer to his age?

Jethro certainly didn't seem to mind what people might think. He turned his head and, finding her attention on him, gave her a smile. "If we d-don't see m-my folks t-today, how fast d-do you think it will t-take the news t-to reach them?"

Knowing the speed of the Amish grapevine, Susannah rolled her eyes. "Probably before we can even get back to the farm."

Jethro nodded in satisfaction.

"You're that eager for them to find out?"

"Ja." His smile migrated from teasing to melancholy. After several minutes with only the sound of the buggy wheels and the cadence of his gelding's hooves on the blacktop, Susannah didn't think Jethro was going to say any more. His gaze was fixed on the road ahead of them, his mind obviously somewhere else.

When he caught her still watching him, Jethro grimaced. "I d-doubt they'll ever stop, b-but I want them t-to consider what they're d-doing a b-bit longer b-before they p-push m-me on the d-district's women again."

Susannah's eyes widened when she watched the strong column of his tanned throat bob in a hard swallow. She heard him clear his throat as he turned his face away. Whatever Jethro was going to say next, it was difficult for him. When he spoke, it was directed toward the far ditch. Sitting breathlessly still, Susannah listened intently, her gaze fixed on the back of the sandy-blond hair that stretched to his shirt collar from under his straw hat.

"I'm… I fear the way you feel about Leroy coming courting is the way…" With his face still turned away, he dipped his chin. His voice dropped in volume so she could barely hear his words. "It's the way women would feel if I came calling."

Her heart clenched. Without thinking, Susannah reached out to grasp the work-roughened hands holding the lines. "Oh *nee*, Jethro. I'm sure that's not true."

Facing forward, his profile revealing a wistful smile, he shrugged one shoulder. "Isn't it?"

"*Nee*. Not that I've been listening to that kind of talk, but I'm sure your courtship would be welcomed."

He snorted softly. "B-because I'm the b-bishop's only son. B-because of the size of m-my farm. B-because I can p-provide for them."

His words struck too close to home for Susannah to immediately respond. Her husband had married her for her farm. And she had done more of the providing. It'd taken a long time to accept that as her primary worth.

Withdrawing her hand, she curled it into a loose fist at the memories. But she couldn't let this *gut*, sensitive man believe that was all he had to offer. She'd been thinking of their subterfuge only as how it might keep her from unwanted courtships. Not how much it might help Jethro avoid the same, potentially painful, activity. Having heard his reluctant admission, Susannah resolved to help protect her self-conscious friend. Even if she'd endure a bit of ridicule herself in doing so. If he wanted a fake sweetheart, she would be one for as long as it lasted.

"You have many more qualities than that. But you'd grow *hochmut* if I sat here listing them all."

"Well, p-proud is one thing I'm not."

"Humility is a quality we should all strive for. And speaking of that, I'm not proud of the way I treated Leroy." Dropping her gaze, Susannah picked absently at a stain in her apron. "I shouldn't have done what I did. I hope *Gott* forgives me for my rudeness." She sighed. "Leroy has some *gut* qualities. They're just… not what I'd look for in a husband."

The squeak of the seat signaled Jethro had shifted his position. She looked up to find him facing her, one sandy-brown brow lifted. "What would you look for in a husband?"

Caught in a trap of her own making, Susannah crossed her arms over her chest. "You think I have a list, like I do with groceries?" When he just smiled, she scowled. "*Ach*, that is difficult, as I'm not looking." She couldn't brush Jethro off when he'd just shared something very personal. Directing her attention to the twitching ears of the bay in front of them, she gave the question serious consideration.

Although affection wasn't the reason they'd married, over the years she and Vernon had grown to love each other in their own ways. But if she were to look for a spouse for reasons other than an imminent need to protect the farm, there were characteristics Vernon hadn't had that Susannah would appreciate. And ones he'd had that she could do without. She supposed that was the way of all married couples. But as for what she'd specifically look for...

"Hardworking." She made a face at her choice of words. "I know that's not the most romantic thing, but... I would appreciate that in a partner."

"Romance? Is that important?"

She shook her head. "*Nee*. Not for me. Romance doesn't get the chores done. Or the fields planted in a timely manner. Besides, I'm too old for romance now."

Jethro thoughtfully ran his fingers through

his short beard. "You think romance is limited t-to the *youngies*? Hmm. I walked in the moonlight last night with a woman who looked just like you. She was skittish about it, b-but I d-don't think she was t-too old for romance."

"She's an old fool if she lets a little moonlit walk turn her head and forget other, more necessary, things regarding a man who's courting her."

"M-must not've b-been you then, 'cause I d-don't see you as old nor a fool, nor ever forgetful of necessary things."

"I should hope not," was all Susannah said, but she fought a blush at his words.

Traffic, both car and buggy, picked up as they approached Miller's Creek. They'd already passed a few buggies going in the opposite direction, the occupants casting them curious looks along with waved greetings. Although resolved to start the charade, Susannah curled her fingers around the edge of the buggy's seat as she pasted a smile on her face. She could feel the weight of all the glances as they drove down the main street.

"If I was courting a woman, I'd p-probably t-take her t-to lunch." Jethro nodded toward the Dew Drop as they approached.

Despite her recent determination, Susannah hesitated. Driving through town in the buggy was one thing, but sitting with him in a restaurant so soon? And taking the time to do so when there was work to be done at home?

Jethro read her reluctance. "P-perhaps another t-time."

Susannah gave him a grateful smile. "I just thought of two more qualities that are *gut* to have in a husband. Thoughtful. And kind. I'm sure many other women would think the same. And you are both of those, Jethro Weaver. In fact, another comes to mind, as well—patient."

"Hardworking and p-patient. I have d-draft horses with those t-traits. M-maybe I'll send them t-to d-do future courting for m-me. B-but they like to eat. And so d-do I. The b-bread and church spread was *gut* earlier, b-but if I d-don't have something m-more soon, m-my stomach will d-do m-most of the t-talking on the way home. If we eat in t-town, you won't have t-to t-take t-time out t-to fix something when we get back. That is, if you were going t-to feed m-me."

She scowled, because he was right. "I'll pick up some deli sandwiches and chips when I'm getting my groceries. Will that do?"

Nodding, he winked at her. Susannah blinked in surprise at the unexpected sight and the absurd breathlessness it caused. When they pulled up in front of the hardware store, she climbed out her side of the buggy as Jethro did, meeting him at the rail provided for Amish customers as he secured the gelding.

"D-do you want to come in with m-me t-to get what's needed for the harness?"

"*Nee*, but I want to make sure I reimburse you for all these parts when you're finished." Skeptical of his innocent look, she furrowed her brow. "I mean it, Jethro. You said a friend was fixing the buggy. I wouldn't take advantage of a friend like that."

"I suppose you're right. If I was getting p-paid in m-meals, that one's thing. B-but it sounds like m-my p-payment is either starvation or a b-bellyache."

Susannah jabbed her elbow into his lean waist. "If it was, it's no more than you deserve. I'm walking down to the Piggly Wiggly to do my shopping."

"Sounds *gut*. This shouldn't t-take long. I'll m-meet you there."

Nodding, she turned away before pivoting to walk backward a few steps. "Do you prefer any particular kind of sandwich and chips?"

"I t-trust you," Jethro replied as he headed into the hardware store.

Susannah pondered his comment as she walked the short distance to the grocery store. She didn't think Jethro trusted easily. Not on things more than sandwiches anyway. He'd placed his trust in her participation of this charade. Whatever came of it, she would ensure he wasn't hurt.

Fifteen minutes later, her gaze was shifting between the two cellophane-wrapped sandwiches in her hands. Turkey and Swiss? Or roast beef and cheddar? Which would Jethro prefer? *Ach,* she might as well get both. Whichever one he didn't want, she'd put it in the refrigerator and Amos would be happy to eat it when he got home from school.

"I heard about your buggy accident! I'm so glad you're all right." Susannah looked up to see a petite, older woman had stopped beside her.

She greeted Naomi, a widowed Amish woman she'd known for decades, with a smile. "*Ja.* It was a bit of an adventure." Susannah didn't elaborate. She intended that no one beyond her and Jethro would know about the nail that'd caused Nutmeg to put them in the ditch. Although most in the community probably already knew she'd let John Schlabach go as her hired man, they could only speculate as to why. She didn't want to cause his *mamm,* Lavinia, any distress. The woman had had enough trouble in her life.

Behind her glasses, Naomi's eyes widened

with curiosity when Jethro stepped up beside Susannah. Aware of the avid attention, Susannah sighed inwardly. *Here we go.* If they wanted to get word out about their "relationship," there wasn't a better place to start. "Which one do you want?" She handed Jethro the sandwiches in her hands. "I couldn't decide."

Jethro debated between the two. "B-both? These and chips will d-do. At least until we get home t-to the cookies that await there." He gave Susannah such a big smile, she bit her cheek to stifle a laugh.

Naomi glanced from him to Susannah's cart. At the collection of ingredients inside, her mouth sagged. "You're baking?" The words were said in the same tone she might have used if Susannah had said she was going to drive trotters in the afternoon's harness races in Milwaukee.

Susannah muzzled her instinctive objection. She could bake, to an extent. But the widow was one of the more acclaimed cooks in the district. And was knowledgeable, even *hochmut*, of the fact, if truth be told. Still contrite over her actions with the widower Leroy, an idea sprang to Susannah.

"You're too right, Naomi. Now that Jethro is joining my family for several meals—" she curled her toes in her tennis shoes at the exaggeration "—he'd probably appreciate it if I improved my skills. If you would have the time, I'd surely appreciate some quick lessons in the kitchen." It was a struggle to get the words out, but Susannah reminded herself it was for a greater purpose.

"Why, of course." Naomi puffed up like the sole rooster in a chicken pen.

"*Denki*. Sometime next week then?"

"*Ja, ja*. Just let me know."

"Oh, I sure will," Susannah assured her. "Are you ready to head home then?" she asked Jethro. With a nod, he put the sandwiches inside the cart and positioned himself to push it. Susannah smiled again at the older woman. "You'll be helping me out considerably, Naomi. I can't thank you enough." Following Jethro to the checkout, she could feel the widow's inquisitive gaze burning through the back of her *kapp*.

"Now we've gone and done it," she muttered to Jethro as they loaded the grocery bags into his buggy.

"I guess it was a successful t-trip into t-town then."

"Did you get what you needed for the harness?"

"That, t-too."

Susannah blew out a breath, not wanting to think about repercussions of what they'd now initiated. "Then I guess we're set."

Lost in their own thoughts as they ate their sandwiches, it was a quiet ride home.

Jethro helped her carry the groceries inside. "Was it as b-bad as you thought?"

"I suppose today was the easy part. Folks who saw us were probably too shocked to say anything. To us, at least," she added wryly.

"Still all right t-to d-do this?"

Although he was trying to hide it, Susannah noted his hopeful expression. "*Ja.* I suppose I don't mind the others talking now. And again when the charade has run its course." A realization had struck today when they'd passed the Dew Drop where Rebecca waitressed. "But what shall I tell my children? I don't want them hurt by this fake relationship." She pressed steepled hands to her chin as she studied Jethro. "I don't want anyone hurt."

"D-do you think they would b-be?"

"I think they enjoyed your company the other night." As did she, but she wasn't going to admit that. "I don't want them to get too hopeful that it's real. Or will become permanent." It was a reminder for herself as well.

Jethro scratched his ear. "I supposed while we coo in p-public, we could argue all the time we're t-together in front of Amos and Rebecca."

"Coo?" She arched her eyebrows. "I'm not quite the cooing sort."

"That's for sure and certain. You're m-more apt to snarl."

"I do not snarl," she retorted.

With a wink and a smile, he climbed into the buggy to drive the gelding to the barn. He paused lifting the lines when she called out to him. "Jethro, most women also appreciate a sense of humor in a man when looking for a husband. I suppose what you have could be called that."

He didn't say anything as he backed the gelding, but Susannah could see the broad grin on his face. A smile on her own, she returned to the house to put up the groceries.

He was still in the barn, presumably repairing the harness when Susannah put on some gear and checked the beehives to ensure they hadn't been bothered by the wasps. From the hill, she saw him emerge from the barn. When Susannah noticed that he was working his way toward the hill, she started down. They met halfway.

"I've got some extra chores at home that have t-to b-be d-done, so I need t-to go."

"I understand. I'm just glad for the help you've provided."

"I m-may not b-be able t-to get b-back for a few d-days as I finish up my field work. I'd b-be glad t-to help you find another hired hand, b-but harvest is a hard t-time of year t-to d-do so. Will you b-be all right?"

"*Ja*. If need be, I'll keep Amos home from school. He's a *gut* student and will quickly catch up." She was oddly reluctant to have him go. "Speaking of field work, do you think we planted enough seed in our little project to get it started?"

"I'd b-be surprised if we d-didn't. Gossip grows like weeds and d-doesn't require m-much cultivation."

They walked in quiet companionship back to the farmyard where she waved him off.

As she put away the limited gear she'd donned for the bees, Susannah wore a pensive smile, considering the man she'd spent a good part of the day with and the discussions they'd had. Her eyes narrowed as she contemplated the qualities she might want in a husband before widening when she realized how many of those characteristics Jethro possessed. Or did Jethro have those qualities and therefore they were the ones she was thinking she'd like in a husband?

Susannah frowned as she strode outside to attack the most strenuous task on her list. Something where she'd need to focus and have very little opportunity to think. Because it was very foolish to be thinking what she was thinking. They had an agreement. It was to be a fake courtship. It certainly wouldn't do to actually consider Jethro as a husband.

Chapter Six

Narrowing his eyes, Jethro leaned forward as he caught sight of a rig approaching on the opposite side of the road. With a huff of disgust, he settled back on his buggy seat. He was acting like a schoolboy, eager at even the possibility of seeing the girl he was sweet on. At his age, he should know better. Their situation wasn't even real. There's no audience that he needed to smile for today. No one to witness his pretend calf eyes. Just because the rig was approaching the crossroad Susannah lived on didn't mean that it would be hers.

Jethro's lips twisted in a self-mocking smile as he focused on the advancing horse, looking for any sign that it might be Nutmeg. At the faint sideways fling of the trotting bay's left front leg, a trait he'd noticed was indicative of

Susannah's mare, his smile widened. It didn't mean that it wasn't, either.

Straightening in the seat, Jethro finally made out a smiling Susannah inside the buggy. His casual return wave as she swung onto the crossroad belied his accelerating pulse. Watching her rig move down the road, he unconsciously turned his gelding down it as well. Cocoa's ears rotated back, as if asking what was going on with the abrupt change of plans. Jethro could understand. He was asking himself the same thing.

Nothing said the only reason he was on this road would be to see Susannah. He hadn't checked on his folks since the day of Susannah's buggy accident. He could probably stop in there. But while Jethro didn't mind his *daed* and *mamm* talking about his rumored romance—as they surely were since the grapevine'd had almost two days to ferment since his and Susannah's trip into town—he didn't want them talking to him about it. At least not yet.

And why couldn't he stop in to see Susannah? They *were* supposedly courting. Although practical Susannah might wonder at his visit. He could always say his reason was that he wanted to see how she was coming along on her harvest with so little help.

As he approached the corner of her property, a reason for stopping suddenly presented itself. Goats. Goats were all over Susannah's farmyard. And based on the burst in speed of her buggy ahead of him, not where they were supposed to be. Jethro clicked Cocoa to a faster pace. When Susannah swept into her lane, he was right behind her.

Drawing the horse to a halt, he quickly set the brake and jumped down from the buggy. Dashing to Susannah's rig, he gave her a hand as she scrambled down as well.

"What happened?"

"I don't know." Her wide-eyed gaze swept over the goats scattered around the farmyard before settling on the pen where creaking hinges bore evidence of the open gate. "They were secured before I left today."

"What d-do you need m-me t-to d-do?"

Sighing, Susannah took stock of all the escaped goats. "If you'd make sure they stay off the road, that would be helpful. I'll get feed and see if I can coax them in. Usually they come running at the sight of the pails."

Nodding, Jethro turned to do as she asked, only to halt in his tracks at her dismayed exclamation. Pivoting, he found Susannah with her lips as compressed as the fists at the ends of her stiff arms.

"What is it?" he urged.

"The bucks are out, too," she muttered, pointing first to a larger spotted goat before moving her finger to indicate another animal, this one roan. "This wasn't an accident. Someone released them." Her voice dropped. Susannah looked more sad than mad at the discovery. Suppressing a surprising urge to reach out in comfort, Jethro kept his arms firmly at his sides.

"*Ach*, I guess I'll be kidding a bit early this year." She looked up at him with a wry smile. "And we'll have to figure out later who is papa to whom."

He frowned in sympathy, knowing she kept careful genetic records. "Will it impact any future sales?"

"It might. Particularly as Eclipse is a La-Mancha breed and Artemis is a Nigerian Dwarf goat."

As no goats were currently inclined to head for the road, Jethro relaxed his stance. Although Susannah seemed more discouraged than upset, Jethro determined his primary task was to cheer her up. "I d-don't understand—" he gestured toward the smooth profile of the larger male goat's head "—why anyone would want a goat without ears."

"They have ears," Susannah mildly chided.

"They're just very small and without cartilage, called 'gopher' ears. I think it makes them distinct. They have a hardy character and *wunderbar* temperament, along with being a solid producing dairy goat with high butterfat content." She smiled. "You should never judge anything by the outward appearance."

Jethro could've lost himself in her brown eyes. He found his hand reaching for her before he jerked it back. She was talking about goats. Not him. He pulled his gaze away. When *Gott* admonished about the dangers of envy, He probably didn't have goats in mind.

With relief, Jethro saw a few of the does working their way across the yard toward the ditch. "I'll keep them off the road. See if the feed works. When we get them in, we'll check if any further d-damage had b-been d-done."

Susannah's smile fell at the reminder that the goats hadn't gotten out by themselves. With a brisk nod, she headed toward the barn. No fools, a couple of the goats already began trailing behind her.

By the time she exited the barn, a red plastic pail in each hand, most of the goats had fortunately congregated in the goat pen. More of them, including the bucks, came trotting through the gate at the sound of feed being poured into the pans strewed about the pen.

Leaving the road, Jethro began working his way toward some of the stragglers. Lifting their heads at his approach, the goats quickly decided the food and the sanctuary in the pen was more appealing than forbidden grazing and the advancing stranger. They scrambled to join the others.

He reached the gate as Susannah was swinging it shut. "Are they all here?"

She ran a silent count as she looked over the multicolored collection of goats in the pen. "*Ja*. Fortunately." Wrapping a chain around the gate, she secured it to the adjacent post.

"You want to sort out the b-bucks now?"

"*Nee*. I'll let them finish eating and settle a bit. Besides, I need to check out their pen and see how they got out."

Jethro tugged on the chain she'd just fastened. It held firmly. He glanced at Susannah. "How d-do you think they got out?"

Susannah pressed her hands over her cheeks. "I can't prove it, but I think John Schlabach, my ex-hired man, let them out." Her shoulders slumped. "It doesn't appear that any of them are hurt, and I'm truly grateful for that. I wish I knew why he was doing this. Even though I had to let him go, I tried to be fair about it." She shook her head dejectedly. "But I recently discovered my timing was truly awful."

They started walking in unison toward the small shed and pasture where Susannah kept the bucks. "His *daed* hit another car while driving drunk and died last weekend. John would've just found out. I'm sure he's upset. I don't know why he put the nail in Nutmeg's collar, but that's probably why he accused me of wanting to shun him like his father was. Apparently he blames that on why Mervin left the community for the *Englisch* when John was a boy. Considering how he was treating his wife, Mervin probably didn't treat John well, either. I recall the older children left home in different ways as soon as possible."

"That d-doesn't change the fact that Mervin was his father. Sometimes feelings for p-parents are...complicated. A child wants to b-be loved no m-matter what a p-p-parent..." It was particularly hard to get the word out. "D-does."

He assumed his *mamm* loved him. At least, he hoped so. Was that the reason he'd always sought her approval? Jethro's lips twisted, making him aware of the numb section where the surgeons had joined his cleft together. He knew she was capable of the emotion, as he'd seen her shower it on his younger brother, Atlee, who'd been killed in a fall during a barn-raising over five years ago. Atlee, who'd left a young wife. Whom Jethro had married, knowing his mother would approve as she'd been the one encouraging it. The only time Jethro had outright contradicted Ruby Weaver was when she'd wanted him to take a secret child Atlee had fathered with a woman other than his wife from the child's mother. He'd refused. The girl and her mother now had a *wunderbar* father and husband in Samuel Schrock.

Jethro scowled as he looked across the field to his folks' farm. His father had been different. Bishop Weaver had been a hard taskmaster, but if you did a job well, he'd give you a nod. It'd been enough. At least it'd been some acknowledgment. The bishop had seemed easier on Atlee when the younger boy had gotten old enough to help. But that could've just been Jethro's perception.

He wasn't going to dwell on it. That was in the past. His gaze slid to the woman walking beside him. He wasn't seeking his parents' approval now. That was for sure and certain.

Susannah's brow was furrowed. "I felt sorry for John. I wanted to help him and Lavinia. Although the community has provided support for her since Mervin left, she's still struggled. I thought the money John brought in would help them both. But it seemed that whatever I told him to do, he wanted to do it a different way.

Or at a different time. I tried to work with that, because, at first, when he would do tasks, he worked hard. But later, even that stopped. It was almost as if he wanted me to notice him defying me. And when he hurt Nutmeg… *Ach,* I couldn't allow that." She shook her head wearily. "He didn't seem surprised when I had to let him go. It was almost as if he thought, since his father had been shunned, then he needed to break the rules as well. If his *daed* was an outcast, then he needed to be, too."

Jethro had no advice to offer. Having no *kinder,* he couldn't say how best to raise them. And he doubted that his childhood was a good example to follow.

Other than a fence panel pulled down, they found no further damage at the bucks' pen. Jethro helped Susannah wire the panel back into place.

After brushing the dirt from her hands, Susannah propped them on her hips and smiled up at him. "I can't thank you enough, Jethro. I'm so glad you stopped by." She tilted her head. "Why did you stop by?"

Jethro deflected the question. "D-do you think he m-might have d-done anything else? The b-bees perhaps?"

Frowning, Susannah took a few quick steps that gave her a better view of the hives on the hill. Shading her eyes with her hand, she scrutinized the area for a long moment before turning back to Jethro. "They look all right from here. I don't think he'd bother them up close. Having been stung a time or two, he was very wary around the bees."

"You want m-me t-to check in the house for you? Will you b-be all right here b-by yourself?"

Susannah shook her head as they turned in that direction. "I'm sure it'll be fine. John wasn't much of one for going into the house, either. And Amos will be home from school soon."

When they returned to the farmyard, Jethro was reluctant to go. At the sound of hoofbeats on the blacktop, they both looked over toward the road.

"It's your folks," Susannah murmured.

Jethro nodded, recognizing his *daed's* horse. "*Gut* thing I'm here then. Support the news I'm sure they've heard around the d-district that we're courting."

"Have they said anything to you yet?"

"*Nee.* B-but I'm sure it's coming soon. You?"

"*Nee.* Unlike you, I don't think they'll speak directly to me about it. I think it's more likely that the bishop will just send more eligible men my way." She bumped him with her hip. "Thanks to your idea about the courtship that's not a courtship, when I say thanks but no thanks, most of them will be easily dissuaded."

At the sight of her teasing grin, it was Jethro's feet—not his speech for once—that stumbled. "Glad it's working out for you."

They both held their breaths as the rig visibly slowed as it approached Susannah's lane. When the buggy crept by the end of the drive, Jethro belatedly lifted his hand to wave. He couldn't see into the shadows of the buggy whether his greeting had been returned. He and Susannah smiled at each other when they simultaneously hissed out an exhale as the rig continued past before increasing speed again.

Watching the buggy crest the hill and drop from sight, Jethro cautioned himself with Susannah's words. *She doesn't want a beau. And even if she did, I wouldn't be on her list of potential candidates.* He needed to keep his heart in check. It reminded him of why he was going into town.

Jethro glanced at the rig he was driving today, the one that had a flat open buckboard extending behind the enclosed driver's seat, the style labeled by the *Englisch* as the Amish pickup truck. He needed some materials to fix a fence. He would do well to keep one around his heart.

"Are you going to the cider frolic tomorrow?"

"D-don't know." He hadn't really thought about it. Although he didn't need any cider, he enjoyed picking apples, and it was a good opportunity to visit with others in the district.

"If you decide not to go, would you mind helping me?"

"Of course. Will you and Amos b-be harvesting? D-do I need to b-bring m-my team?"

"*Nee.* Just your arms and your patience." Susannah's eyes were sparkling.

Jethro's mouth grew dry at the sight. He knew what he'd like to do with his arms. Put them around her. He bit down hard on his tongue. *Fences, remember?* Apparently he couldn't erect them fast enough. He cleared his throat. "I d-don't understand?"

"My *dochder* Rachel hasn't been out much since she had the babies a few weeks ago. I'm going to watch them so she, Ben and their hired girl can go to the frolic, along with Amos and Rebecca. I need your help with the twins."

His help with the twins? His heart lurched with trepidation tangled with longing at the prospect. Any hope of a child in his life had been lost when his pregnant wife had died. At the thought of a baby in his arms, Jethro knew it wasn't just fences he needed to erect around his heart. It was walls.

Chapter Seven

Any trepidation Jethro felt about the after-noon was eased when he stepped through the door the next day. Glancing around Susan-nah's kitchen, he wondered if the goats had gotten out again and invaded the house this time. "D-do you need some help?"

"Now why would you ask that?" Susannah's tone was as crisp as the black-edged cookies on the nearby cooling rack.

"I suppose it's b-because it looks like you d-do? Or m-maybe b-because I know you d-don't have enough t-time t-to keep running into t-town for ingredients that d-don't end up very—" He touched one of the cookies on the rack. It disintegrated under his finger. "Use-ful."

"*Ach*, Amos wore out the knees on his pants. They were getting too short anyway. I was working on some new ones for him while these were in the oven. I fear I was sewing seams when I should've been watching the time." Her shoulders slumped, along with her expression. "I told Rachel I'd have something for her to take when she dropped off the *boppeli* and now I'm behind."

"And she agreed t-to t-take them?" Jethro couldn't help himself. It felt *gut* to be able to tease. The concept of joking with his *mamm* or deceased wife would've been like trying to milk a goose. Ridiculous and uncomfortable for all parties.

Susannah turned away from the counter to give him a mock glare. The effect was spoiled by the faint traces of flour along one side of her hairline.

"What can I d-do to help?" Crossing to the sink, Jethro washed his hands in preparation.

"Run to the store for me and buy some?"

He laughed then stepped up beside her. "You can d-do it. I'll m-measure and you d-dump and stir. Where's your recipe?"

Susannah tapped an index card lying on the counter, its surface stained with spatters of long gone baking episodes. Jethro ran his finger down the list of ingredients. Since the butter and eggs were already out, he searched the cupboard from where she'd pulled the wasp supplies days ago for the rest of what he was looking for and set them on the counter.

Susannah plunked a few measuring cups down on his side of a large bowl before selecting a wooden spoon from a collection of similar cooking utensils in an upright canister on the counter. Measuring out the butter, he handed it to Susannah. While she whipped it vigorously, he dumped the appropriate amount of sugar into the bowl.

"Ach!" She shot him a frown as, still stirring, she slid the bowl farther down the counter.

Preparing the next sequence of recipe items, Jethro raised an eyebrow. *"You* of all p-people are going t-to b-be p-picky about how the ingredients are added? D-don't you t-trust m-me?"

With an exaggerated sigh, she scooted the bowl closer again, and he added those ingredients as well, albeit more slowly. "B-besides, it's not as if folks have high expectations for any b-baked goods of yours."

Susannah huffed softly. "Well then, it's time I surprise them."

"Oh, with what's running along the grapevine about us, I'm sure we're already d-doing that." Rescanning the card, he measured the rest of the ingredients, checking with Susannah for approval to add them before he did so. When everything was in the batter, he put the supplies away while she continued to stir. Using the side of a hand, Jethro slid a small heap of flour, left over from her earlier efforts, off the counter into the palm of his other cupped hand. "You're a m-messy cook."

Leaving the spoon in the bowl, Susannah dusted her hands off on her apron. Jethro gently snagged one to turn it palm up. With a smile, his eyes met her soft brown ones as he deposited the residue from his cupped hand into it. His smile faded as their fingers tangled. Susannah's lips parted, drawing his attention.

Jethro ached to kiss them. His chin dipped. He froze. He'd never kissed a woman other than Louisa. And that was only once. Conscious of the numbness of the scarred section of his lips, he'd been self-conscious about kissing. Louisa's reaction to his one attempt reinforced that he'd had reason to be. It might've been his kiss. It might've just been him. He hadn't been her choice, after all. Either way, he couldn't bear to see the same reaction on Susannah's face. Clearing his throat, Jethro withdrew his hand and stepped back.

He winced as some of the debris between their hands scattered to the linoleum. "I'll sweep that up." Striving to clear the sudden tension that pervaded the room, Jethro retrieved a broom and a dustpan from a tall, narrow cupboard as he tried to remember what he'd said just before…before he'd almost made a huge fool of himself. "Knowing you're so m-meticulous about everything on the farm, the state of the kitchen surprises m-me."

Having emptied what was in her hand into the trash, along with the burned cookies from the last batch, Susannah was now spooning dough onto cookie sheets. She tilted her head as her brow furrowed. Jethro hoped she was thinking about his question rather than his near blunder.

"I think it's because the farm was my *daed's* and my domain. I didn't spend much time in the kitchen with my *mamm* and older *schweschdere*. I learned we might live in the house, but our livelihood came from the farm. After my *daed* died, the farm was passed down to me as the youngest. I appreciated that Vernon tolerated my lack of enthusiasm for housework, understanding I'd rather be outside working, though I suppose he should've, as he married me for it. But then, there were other things he'd rather be doing than farming as well. Fortunately, Rachel and Rebecca enjoyed working in the house, so some semblance of order was maintained and we didn't starve."

She put the cookie sheets into the oven.

Glancing outside when something caught his attention in the window, Jethro saw a horse and buggy arrive. "D-does Rachel know? About us? About what we want folks to think of us, I mean?" Jethro hastily corrected himself.

Susannah watched her *dochder* descend from the buggy. "*Nee*. She's not a gossiper, neither is Ben. But she might unintentionally mention you are here today."

"That's what we want, right?"

Although she hesitated a moment, Susannah nodded. "*Ja*. That's what we want."

Jethro's stomach twisted. He read in her expression that any wanting regarding their relationship would be more he, than we.

By the time Rachel came inside like a whirlwind, her arms full with twins, the cookies were out of the oven and cooling on racks. Rachel's husband, Ben, was a step behind, carrying a handmade bag of baby supplies, while Miriam Schrock, their hired girl—as was Amish custom to help a new mother for a while—smiled from the doorway.

"Are you sure you don't want to come with us today?" her *dochder* asked with the breathlessness of a new mother coordinating an outing with two infants.

Ja, Susannah was sure. She wasn't ready to face all the eyes of the district on her and Jethro, now that word was surely out about their relationship. After the recent, unexpected moment in the kitchen when their hands had touched, she was afraid she'd blush like a *maedel* if anyone glanced at the two of them. Which was ridiculous, as she wasn't a young girl anymore, they hadn't done anything, and this whole thing was just a ruse.

"Most definitely," she assured Rachel, relieving her daughter of her grandson, Eli. "I've been to many cider frolics, but I've never before had a chance to watch my *kinskinder* for the afternoon."

"Are you sure you can handle them by yourself?"

Susannah arched an eyebrow at Rachel. "I've handled a *boppeli* or two before. And I won't be by myself. I have help." Susannah pivoted to thrust Eli into Jethro's arms. At the sight of his wide eyes and dropped jaw, she couldn't prevent the smile that curved her lips as she turned back to take Amelia from her daughter's hands.

"If you're sure?" Rachel's curious gaze

shifted between Susannah and a stunned Jethro, who now held her infant son.

"I'm sure. Now go enjoy." Although she gazed down into her granddaughter's sleeping face, in her peripheral vision Susannah could see Ben's callused hand clasp around Rachel's slender one. Her smile widened at the action. An expectant couple with a surprise marriage, Ben and Rachel had struggled during the early months of their union. Although confident they'd work it out—they had to, as Amish didn't believe in divorce—Susannah was thrilled to see them getting along so well now. Always elated to see her twin grandchildren, Susannah was also glad to give their parents a chance to socialize as a couple.

"They ate just before we came. I should be back in a few hours. But I packed bottles for them just in case they get hungry." Pulling them out of the bag, Rachel put them into the refrigerator.

"I'm sure we'll be fine. Won't we, Jethro?" Susannah swiveled to look at her pretend suitor, in part to ensure he was doing all right with the unexpected babe. When she saw the pair, her breath caught in her throat at the tender expression worn by the bearded man as he gazed at the infant. Jethro didn't look up at her question. Throat suddenly clogged with an emotion she couldn't define, Susannah had to clear it as she turned back to her daughter. "We'll be fine," she repeated hoarsely.

She tipped her head toward the cookies on the counter. "Don't forget to take those. They just need packing up."

At her mother's request, Rachel automatically extended the hand not entwined with her husband's toward the cookies. Casting a dubious glance at them, she hesitated. "Are you sure?"

Susannah grasped at the chance to regain equilibrium shaken by the sight of Jethro with the *boppeli*. She rolled her eyes. "After all those years of living with me, you should've realized by now that I know my own mind. *Ja*. I'm sure. But to protect your reputation in the community, you can announce to everyone that you didn't make them, I did. And they're delicious." Susannah bit her cheek at the exaggeration. "Jethro helped me with them. We're a *gut* team."

Rachel fixed Susannah with such a warm look that Susannah wondered if it'd been intended for the babe in her arms instead of her. "*Ja*. I can see that you are, *Mamm*." Her quiet murmur caused the flush Susannah had been hoping to avoid earlier to blossom across her cheeks. She needn't have worried. Rachel had already shifted her attention to efficiently packing up the cookies. "Where are Amos and Rebecca?"

"They didn't know if you'd have room in the buggy. Besides, I think they both wanted to get there early in order to spend as much time with their friends as possible."

Rachel nodded. Handing the cookies to Ben, she tenderly stroked a finger down the cheek of each of her sleeping *boppeli*.

"We'll be fine," Susannah reassured her yet again.

With a final wave, Rachel and Ben followed Miriam out of the kitchen. It seemed unnaturally quiet as the door swung shut behind them.

Braced this time for the disconcerting impact the man holding the infant gave her, Susannah looked at Jethro. "She didn't leave us any cookies."

Jethro lifted his gaze from the baby and smiled. "Is that *gut* or b-bad?"

"It would've been nice to taste them. Just in case."

"You have t-to t-trust us, Susannah. As you said, we m-make a *gut* t-team."

"Well, I appreciate your help today, as these two definitely take a team." She smiled as she recalled that Jethro, neighbor of Rachel and

Ben, had been the one to come get her the night the twins had arrived. He hadn't stayed to see them then. In fact, this might be the first time he'd been around a small babe.

"Shall we sit down?" She nodded toward the chairs in the living area. "One thing I always want to enjoy and never take for granted is holding a *boppeli*."

As she eased into her rocker with the baby in her arms, what felt like a rock settled in her stomach. She'd forgotten that Jethro had never had a chance to hold his infant child. It'd been lost, along with his wife, before it was born. Her stark gaze fastened on the man settling into a nearby chair. "Oh, Jethro. I'm so sorry. I didn't think…"

He lifted his eyes from the sleeping boy. "It was *Gott's* will. Although I…" He dropped his attention back to the infant. "It wouldn't have mattered, but I sometimes wonder if the child had…" Careful not to disturb the baby he cuddled, he touched the scar on his upper lip with his free hand. "I worried about giving that to any children. It…wasn't always easy."

Susannah's eyes closed as she thought of the babies, the two she'd lost due to what she and her husband passed on to them. The Amish had begun with a limited number of families. Due to the requirement of being baptized into the church to be married, over the generations, the gene pool had narrowed. Recessive hereditary diseases were showing up in their children. Ones like the Crigler-Najjar syndrome, a genetic disorder causing severe jaundice that her affected babies hadn't survived.

When the infant shifted in her arms, Susannah opened her eyes to take in Amelia's thankfully beautiful skin. As if to reassure her *grossmammi*, the infant momentarily blinked open her clear blue eyes before they disappeared again under fluttering fragile lashes.

"Is it genetic?" she asked quietly.

"I don't know."

They lapsed into silence. Susannah didn't know if Jethro had noticed, but his stuttering was diminished as he held her grandson. Were his thoughts on that? Or were his thoughts, like hers, on the genetic issues both of them had witnessed in their community? Her gaze focused on Amelia's tiny perfect fingers, curled into a little fist that rested against her cheek as she slept. Perhaps Jethro was thinking about the wonder of *Gott's* creation that a *boppeli* was?

A wonder that she would experience now as a *grossmammi*, not a *mamm*. It was enough. It was more than enough.

She glanced at Jethro through lowered lashes.

He was a compelling sight with the child in his arms. It was a *gut* thing their courtship wasn't real. If they were to get married, there might be a possibility of little ones as, with children being a gift from *Gott*, their church didn't believe in birth control. It would be *Gott's* will, but would there be more heartbreaking issues like the ones they'd already experienced?

Susannah knew Amish women who'd had babes in their later years. She also knew risk factors increased with age, for the mother and the child. Her arms tightened around her granddaughter. She couldn't bear to lose another baby. Her arms and her heart had felt devastatingly empty after the two she'd lost. To remarry, and risk losing more? It didn't bear thinking about. To take her mind off the disturbing direction, she asked the first thing that popped into her head.

"Is the cleft related to your…" She hesitated to bring up his speech. It'd never been an issue to her, but she knew it was to him.

"Stammer? I don't think so. When I was in school, it was b-before they'd built the Amish one, so, like you, I went to the p-public school. B-because of my stammer, I saw a speech pathologist." His brow creased slightly in reflection. "She helped me a lot."

"Did it ever go away?" After Susannah was

married, she'd been so busy with the farm and her own young family, she hadn't had time to interact with the neighbor boy she'd once babysat.

"*Nee.* B-but it got m-much better. Until I left school after eighth grade and didn't work with her anymore."

"Who was it?"

"Mrs. D-Danvers," he said with a faint smile.

Susannah's instantly pictured an older *Englisch* woman. "I remember her. She's retired now. I see her sometimes in town. Maybe she'd work with you again?"

Jethro's smile faded. He gave a barely discernible shake of his head, his focus returning to the baby in his arms. Susannah's breath caught at the tenderness in his expression. If she could make a secret list of character traits she'd like in a husband, tenderness would definitely be one of them.

"*Nee.* It is what it is. I'd rather just keep my words few since it t-takes me t-twice as long to say them. Save them mainly for m-my livestock and close friends." His gaze briefly lifted to meet Susannah's.

Warmed more than she should be by the obvious inclusion in that category, Susannah dropped her own gaze to watch as sleeping Amelia scrunched up her face before the tiny rosebud lips curved into a smile. Concerned that the sensations that flowed through her were way too cozy and tempting, Susannah sought a topic to stop the wayward emotions in their tracks.

"Your *daed* has been bishop here a long time, *ja*?"

Jethro frowned. "Since just b-before I was b-born, I understand."

"He must've been very young when he was chosen."

"*Ja.* I heard he became a m-minister shortly after he was b-baptized and m-married, and when the b-bishop d-died the following year, m-my *d-daed* was selected to replace him." Jethro inhaled deeply.

Susannah winced inwardly as his speech tightened up again.

"Knowing that I was also agreeing to serve as leader if selected was the only thing that m-made m-me hesitate about b-baptism into the church. I hold m-my b-breath every election, hoping *Gott* d-doesn't choose m-me. Although I d-don't know why He would, when folks would surely rather watch a field of alfalfa grow than listen t-to m-me t-try t-to p-preach."

Susannah smiled. While church members chose the nominees, *Gott* chose the minister from the nominees by determining who would pick up the *Ausbund* hymnal containing a scripture verse. The lifelong job was rarely sought and although it was considered an honor to be chosen, she'd seen grown men sob with dismay when a hymnal was opened and revealed as the one containing scripture. She couldn't imagine what the task of preaching for twenty minutes to an hour without notes on a regular basis would do to Jethro.

What she *could* imagine, as she watched him totally absorbed by the infant he cradled, was Jethro as a father. He would be a *wunderbar* one. With a surprising pang, she shifted so she could rest the arm holding Amelia against the extension of the chair. The babe, although weighing but a few pounds, grew surprisingly heavy in an unsupported arm. A bit like her heart as she considered the man across from her. *Ja*, it was a good thing their courtship wasn't real. Jethro needed a family she couldn't give him. Closing her eyes to what had suddenly become a painful sight, Susannah hoped for him that he would find someone who could. Pressing her free hand against her stomach, she attempted to stifle the regret that immediately pooled there at the thought.

Chapter Eight

The bishop had obviously pressed Leroy Albrecht to call on her again. Susannah wasn't surprised. Bishop Weaver surely knew now of her and Jethro's courtship and wanted to ensure his neighbor didn't get any ideas about a permanent relationship with his only son. Instead of confronting it head-on, Bishop Weaver seemed intent on sending more suitable candidates in her direction.

A couple of them had stopped by a few days ago on Visiting Sunday. Susannah felt no compunction on gently dissuading them by indicating she was seeing someone else. She was. Just not seeing him all the way to matrimony. And these were nice men. But not ones she saw herself marrying, even if she were looking. If she ever changed her mind, it wouldn't do to burn any bridges in case later they were the only ones to cross the void. Although Susannah didn't feel a void now, when Amos was grown and in charge of the farm, it might be nice to have some companionship.

But regarding Leroy, she wanted him to come over. At the appropriate time. Unsurprisingly, he'd been very reluctant when she'd issued the invitation. That was why she appreciated the bishop's pressure in his case. Without it, Leroy might not've grudgingly accepted.

Although Susannah didn't bring many desserts to community gatherings, she had definitely helped serve her share. Just as she noted any nuances of her goats' behavior while feeding them in case one was sick or needed attention, she was very observant when feeding others as well. In fact, she'd noticed more than once that Naomi had discreetly placed extra servings of desserts next to Leroy at the meals on church Sundays since shortly after the man had been widowed. Leroy had noticed the food, but not who'd nudged the plates near him. Susannah figured it was long past time Naomi got credit for her efforts. She also figured Naomi wouldn't mind someone who truly appreciated her skills in the kitchen sitting at her table on a regular basis.

At the sound of a muted clatter, Susannah looked out the window to see Leroy's rig coming up the lane. "Looks like we have some company," she chirped as she whipped a wooden spoon more quickly around the bowl of cake batter, the pace in sync with her accelerated heart rate.

"Oh, were you expecting anyone?" Naomi asked, as she was dusting a cake pan farther down the counter.

"*Nee*, good thing you brought over an example of what a *gut* dessert should look like." Fixing an encouraging smile at the widow, Susannah hoped her plan would work. She didn't know how many more visits she—or Leroy—could take. Or how much more time she could waste in her kitchen when the farm needed her elsewhere.

Naomi rose on her tiptoes to look out the window. "Leroy Albrecht is here?" Her question, accompanied by a faint blush, ended with a squeak. She glanced at Susannah. Her narrowed gaze seemed to ask, *How many men do you need to come courting?*

Sliding damp palms down the sides of her apron, Susannah crossed to the front door. Pinning on a bright smile, she opened it to see Leroy sitting in his buggy, wearing a morose expression as he stared at the house. Upon seeing her, his shoulders lifted in what she assumed as a sigh—either that or a fortifying breath. Slowly climbing down from the buggy, he secured his horse to the rail and plodded to the door at a pace that suggested he'd rather be any place else.

"Leroy." She ushered him through the door. "How pleasant to see you today." For the first time since she'd noticed the man's gaze on her, Susannah meant it. "I've been baking. It'll take a few minutes, but I can treat you to a warm spice cake."

Leroy froze in his tracks, preventing Susannah from shutting the door. His face paled. "I… I don't know that I'll be able to stay that long."

"You'll at least have time for a cup of *kaffi* since you came all this way." Her plan wouldn't work if she couldn't get him through the door. Placing a firm but gentle hand on his shoulder, Susannah urged him toward the table. "And, if you don't have time to wait, Naomi, would you mind cutting into that streusel cake you brought over? It would go wonderfully with *kaffi*. I'll just get some plates out."

Susannah scooted over to the cupboard to retrieve two plates. Setting them on the table, along with a couple of forks, she returned to where she'd left the bowl on the counter. "Naomi," she said over her shoulder, "why don't you sit for a minute and keep Leroy company while I finish this up?"

Her hands slowly stirring the cake batter, Susannah kept her ears tuned to any sounds behind her. When she heard the first, then the second, chair move on the linoleum floor, she exhaled inaudibly in relief. At the continued silence, other than the quiet *tink* of a fork against china, she turned to the two seated at the table. "So how is it?" she inquired cheerfully.

Leroy's plate of cake was already half empty. His eyes were closed in blissful appreciation as he slowly chewed. "Mmm." He opened them to stare at the intently watching woman on the other side of the table. "This is *wunderbar*." Under his gaze, Naomi flushed rosily as she reached up to tuck her gray-threaded hair under her *kapp*.

"Naomi is one of the best bakers in the district. Has been for some time. I imagine you've sampled some of her desserts before at church dinners. But then, maybe not. If you don't eat early or have someone hold a piece back for you, there generally isn't any left." Susannah bit the inside of her cheek. She felt like an auctioneer at a mud sale, keeping up a patter to encourage bidders.

"If I haven't before, I'll be sure not to miss them now." Leroy took another bite, his eyes closing again in obvious approval. "This is how a wife should be able to bake."

Susannah turned back to scowl at the batter in the bowl before her. Keeping her actions quiet so as not to disturb the couple behind her, she slid the prepared cake pan closer and poured the batter into it.

"My Absalom was very happy with my baking. His favorite was my shoofly pie. He liked it even better than this streusel cake."

That a way, Naomi, Susannah silently cheered at the older woman. Stealing a glance at the table, she hid a smile as Leroy served himself another piece.

"I'd be happy to try it sometime," the widower mumbled around another forkful.

"I'd bake more, but when I don't have a purpose to bake for, it takes some of the enjoyment from it. It's no fun baking for one. And, lately, it's challenging to get things done outside. Even with my small place, by the time I feed the horse and care for his needs, along with other tasks, it doesn't leave me much time in the kitchen, which is where I'd rather be. And speaking of my horse, I've been having a problem with him lately."

Tuned in to the conversation behind her rather than the cake she was sliding into the oven, Susannah raised her eyebrows. Perhaps

Naomi didn't need her help, after all. The widow seemed to be doing fine on her own. But just in case, Susannah inserted, "Leroy is a *wunderbar* horseman. Just ask him."

And so Naomi did. While the two at the table discussed the merits of Standardbreds purchased from the track versus those raised for Amish buggy work, and the decision to shoe horses one way as opposed to another, Susannah cleared up the counter.

"Sure would be nice to have someone so knowledgeable take a look at my gelding," Naomi sighed at the end of one of Leroy's monologues.

Susannah figured that was as good a nudge as any. Opening the oven door, she peered at the underdone cake. "This should be out soon and we can sample it as well. Of course, it'll be nowhere near to Naomi's, but I've been working on it and I'm sure…"

Leroy's chair scraped back from the table. Brushing cake crumbs from his graying beard, he hastily stood. "Well, I need to be going. Got things to do, you know. Just thought I'd drop by." He smiled at Naomi and even Susannah had to admit it made him look almost appealing. Almost.

To Naomi, the expression must've been considerably appealing indeed. She shot a beseeching glance at Susannah. Hastily interpreting it, Susannah shut the oven door with her hip and crossed her arms over her chest, mostly to hold in her laughter. "*Ach*, that's too bad. If I remember correctly, didn't you mention, Naomi, that you wouldn't be able to stay long today, either?"

The widow beamed as she pushed back from the table as well. "*Ja, ja.* I've got to be going as well. Chores, you know."

Leroy paused at the door. "Well, I suppose I could follow you home and see what issues you might be having with your horse."

Susannah quickly returned the rest of Naomi's cake to its traveling container. She thrust it and its contents into the widower's unresisting hands. "Why don't you take this along and enjoy it while you discuss those issues. In a few minutes my own cake will be out, which is more sweets than I need. Unless you'd like to take some of that along as well?"

She smiled as the older pair made hasty goodbyes and fled from the kitchen.

Snagging a spatula, she scraped the bowl before putting it in the sink. With a finger, Susannah swiped some batter from the spatula, tasting it thoughtfully as she watched Leroy help Naomi into her buggy. Considering her skill set in the kitchen, it was not bad work for an afternoon. Not bad at all.

Susannah carried two baskets loaded with jars of honey into the Dew Drop the next day. Her eyes swept the interior of the restaurant, which contained only a scattering of customers in the midafternoon. Recalling Rebecca's comments about the restaurant's potential sale, Susannah's hands tightened on the basket's handles. The Dew Drop was a much needed outlet for her honey and other items. Hopefully, the new owners would continue to allow her to sell them here.

Rebecca waved to her from where she was clearing a table. Nodding in return, Susannah set the baskets on the floor and began to restock the shelf space allotted to her in the wooden cupboard by the checkout counter. Thrilled that sales for herself, as well as some of the other local Amish craftsmen she shared the cupboard with, had been good this fall, she quickly emptied one basket and started on the other. Having placed all from the second basket that would fit on the shelf, Susannah gave the display a final satisfied survey before grabbing the handles and glancing around the restaurant for a quick farewell to her daughter.

Not seeing Rebecca, she shrugged and strode toward the door.

Before she reached it, it swung open to admit a quartet of older *Englisch* women. Although she hadn't had any of them in the limited years that she'd gone to the local public school, Susannah recognized them as teachers, apparently retired by now. Among them was Mrs. Danvers, the speech teacher whom Jethro had mentioned as being such a help to him in his early years. Appreciative of what the woman had done then for the shy young boy he would've been, Susannah gave the woman a smile and brief nod. To her dismay, while the other three drifted on to a table, Mrs. Danvers paused in front of Susannah.

"Mrs. Mast?"

Susannah hesitantly nodded acknowledgment.

"You probably don't know me. I used to teach in the public school system, dating back to when the Amish children in the area attended before they set up their own school." The older woman smiled, her face creasing in graceful lines. "I've tried to keep track of some of those previous students. One of those that I had was Jethro Weaver. I understand you two have been seeing each other recently."

Susannah's eyes widened at the woman's

comments. One of Jethro's and her objectives was for their artificial courtship to be discussed along the Amish grapevine. She never imagined it would make the jump to an *Englisch* one.

Mrs. Danvers reached out to gently pat one of Susannah's hands curled around the basket handle. "He was one of my favorite students. Such an earnest, hardworking boy."

Smiling faintly at the image of Jethro around her son Amos's age, Susannah had to agree. "*Ja.* He was just speaking last week of what a huge help you were to him back then." Encouraged by the woman's warm expression, she continued, figuring that as Jethro held his former teacher in high opinion, he wouldn't mind if she shared their conversation. "He said he spoke better when you were working with him."

Mrs. Danvers' smile ebbed. "I was afraid that might've been the case. Although he did well in our sessions and his teachers at the time said there was much improvement, I don't think he had much encouragement at home."

The woman's observation didn't surprise Susannah at all. She hadn't witnessed that Jethro'd had much encouragement at home, regardless of the topic.

"I worked with him for a number of years.

Due to issues from the cleft lip and palate as well as the stutter. Children born with clefts frequently need SLT." At Susannah's blank look, the older woman's smile reappeared. "I'm sorry. After years in the field, the lingo just slips out. Speech and language therapy."

"Is stuttering common with clefts?"

"No, not really. One of the reasons I would've liked to have spoken with his parents at some point. Stuttering tends to run in families. It would've been interesting to know if anyone in their family stuttered."

Susannah blinked in surprise. "Stuttering does? I assumed maybe clefts were but not the other."

"There are some genetic relationships in both." Mrs. Danvers acknowledged her companions, who were now waving at her from their table. "I enjoy getting out with friends, but I have plenty of free time. I'd be happy to work with Jethro again if he'd like."

"Oh, that isn't for me to say. You'd have to ask Jethro." Susannah's response was instantaneous. Jethro had said as much. He was sensitive about his stutter and valued his privacy. But…what if working with the speech teacher again for a while would help him? She'd witnessed how, when he was more relaxed, as he'd been holding the babe, the stutter was diminished. Maybe this would help him when their charade was over. Susannah felt a pang at the thought. She really was enjoying Jethro's company. Their agreement was for the short term as Jethro didn't want to face courting anyone right now. But with a newfound confidence, he might not find it so onerous. She wanted that for him.

"Wait. *Ja.* That might be *gut.* He is a fine man just the way he is. But being able to speak better, or be more relaxed when he speaks, might help him in…other ways." She couldn't say "in self-confidence." That would seem to be intruding on Jethro's privacy. Hopefully, Mrs. Danvers, with her years of knowledge on the topic, would understand what she meant.

The older woman's compassionate smile indicated she did.

"Denki so much for what you've done for him."

"It's no problem. As I said, he was one of my favorite students." With a small nod, Mrs. Danvers went to join the three other women.

Susannah watched her thoughtfully as the woman reached their table. With a shrug, she slid the basket handles up her arm, exited the restaurant and stepped directly into the path of Ruby Weaver, the bishop's wife—and Jethro's *mamm.*

Chapter Nine

Susannah halted so abruptly the basket handles slid down her arms. Only a frantic grab prevented them from tumbling onto the sidewalk along with the few jars of honey that remained in one.

Ruby Weaver stopped as well, her blue eyes raking Susannah from her *kapp* down to her tennis shoes. Susannah had never noticed that Jethro's were the same color. His were so warm and kind while his mother's seemed cold and flat. The realization helped Susannah rein in her galloping heart rate at the unexpected meeting. If his folks were unhappy with their supposed relationship, it was no more than what she and Jethro had expected. Remembering this was for him, Susannah straightened. And smiled.

"*Guder daag*, Ruby." Accustomed to working with livestock and having recently been stung by wasps, Susannah knew enough to be wary of unpredictable creatures. A category that included the bishop's wife. Hoping to escape with the simple "good day," Susannah continued toward her nearby buggy.

"Is that what you're catching him with?"

Inhaling slowly as she kept her smile on her face, Susannah turned around. "Pardon?"

"Honey." The woman nodded her head at the remaining jars in one of the baskets. But her gaze on Susannah indicated the word had nothing to do with what a bee provided and everything to do with what she thought Susannah was granting to her son to entice his attentions.

Susannah would've laughed at the insinuation if it hadn't been so insulting. Her smile turned rueful as she regarded the older woman. "You obviously don't know your son." Cocking her head, Susannah held Ruby's frowning stare as she recalled the young Jethro she'd cared for and the current one she was beginning to care for in a much different way. Even though their courtship wasn't real, she wasn't going to let this woman denigrate Jethro. "Perhaps you never did. Which is your loss. He is a *gut* man and a dutiful son. One you don't deserve. The man he's become is more credit to him than you."

Ruby's eyes narrowed and her mouth puckered like she'd taken a gulp of Susannah's vinegar-infused lemonade. Shaking her head sadly, Susannah continued to her buggy, opened the door and stored her baskets on the floor.

"You don't deserve him, either."

She wasn't surprised to hear the words behind her. Slowly pivoting, she found Ruby had followed her to the edge of the sidewalk. "You're probably right about that. But he's a grown man and it's for him to decide, ain't so?"

Maybe this time he wants to choose his own wife instead of having his parents force a bride upon him once again. Susannah bit her tongue to keep the words from escaping her mouth.

Suddenly having no more energy for the conversation—she'd already said more than she should—she yanked the lead loose from the hitching post, causing Nutmeg to fling up her head in surprise. Instantly contrite, Susannah crooned an apology to the mare. Making a point to control her movements—she refused to give the impression she was intimidated or running away—she climbed into the buggy. With a stiff nod to the still watching woman,

Susannah backed Nutmeg onto the street and headed home.

She was disgusted to find herself still shaking a full block away. *You've gone and done it now.* She'd never crossed the bishop's wife before. She'd never really crossed anyone before. *If Ruby wasn't upset initially, ach, you put her well on her way there.*

Susannah's lips twisted. *I wonder if Jethro can court me if his parents find some reason to put me in the Bann?*

It was a possibility. It hadn't happened in their district, although Bishop Weaver— frequently prompted by his wife—could be strict. But Susannah had heard stories from others that in dysfunctional churches, leaders had shunned members for personal reasons. Women for not having their *kapps* made correctly. Or having hair that frizzed and wouldn't lay down flat enough under their head covering. So it could happen. Susannah was more worried about what being in the *Bann* would do to Amos and Rebecca than to her relationship with Jethro. If she was shunned, she couldn't eat at the same table as them. Or take anything from their hand. They would be greatly distressed, as would she.

Her trembling finally ceased a mile out of town when she determined that Bishop Weaver and Ruby surely knew Jethro enough to realize that—dutiful son not withstanding—shunning the unsuitable woman he was courting would only push him further in that direction. Finally relaxed as she turned down the road toward her farm, Susannah shook her head. All this emotion for a relationship that wasn't real to begin with. Although, her fingers twitched on the leather lines, as often as she was seeing Jethro, it was feeling more real all the time.

And if it really was real, then she'd have Ruby Weaver as a mother-in-law. Susannah almost giggled at the thought. Wouldn't that be something? They would surely clash on occasion. On *many* occasions. They wouldn't find her frail like Jethro's first wife. Would the bishop and his wife go so far as to try to put their own daughter-in-law in the *Bann* if she crossed them, unintentionally or not? What would the district think of that? *Gut* thing their courtship wasn't real. And why did that acknowledgment make her feel a little wistful?

Jethro unhitched Cocoa from his buggy and led the gelding to where his father's rig was parked by the barn. He'd kept a wary eye on the house as he'd driven up the lane, bracing himself for the kitchen door to swing wide and his *mamm* or *daed*, or most likely both, would stomp out of their house to give him the lecture he was sure they felt was needed.

When the door didn't open and a scan of the farmyard revealed his *mamm's* buggy was missing, he breathed a little easier. A peek through the large open barn doors confirmed it held no occupants other than a slouch-hipped bay in the stall and a yellow-and-white cat curled up on a hay bale. As both their attentions were turned toward the back of the barn, Jethro paused to peer into the shadows as well.

Seeing nothing, he smiled faintly. He couldn't have picked a better time to check on the issue his *daed* had mentioned he was having with his buggy when he'd seen him briefly in town. His father, wearing a frown, had stopped him yesterday outside the hardware store. Jethro had been afraid the discussion he'd been expecting but trying to avoid—his unacceptable courtship of Susannah—was about to begin. He'd looked around with dread, afraid of someone overhearing the lecture. His knees had almost sagged when his father had asked if he'd take a look at his buggy, which had been pulling oddly.

Distracted by relief and an immediate interruption by a church member, Jethro hadn't been able to interpret the problem based on the bishop's short description. He'd determined to take the rig for a drive today to get a better idea of the issue. At least then he'd know what to fix. A last glance around the barn confirmed the bay horse and cat as his only company while fixing the buggy. He much preferred their company to his folks', who would be leaning over his shoulder, haranguing him on how he should fix his life to suit them while he tried to do the repairs.

Jethro eyeballed the buggy as he hitched up his gelding. Other than expected wear in some areas, he couldn't see anything obvious prior to climbing into the buggy.

As he drove down the lane, ears tuned to any sounds the conveyance might be making, Jethro reflected that his ability with repairs was something he'd at least felt was appreciated while he was growing up. His father wasn't good with mechanics, proclaiming his talents lay elsewhere. Jethro didn't know if his *daed* meant that his skills were more people-related.

Recalling some memories of his youth, Jethro snorted. He didn't see that, either. He supposed there were others in the community who'd disagree, thinking the bishop was doing a good job. The role, one his father had been in for longer than he could remember, certainly rested easily on his father's shoulders.

Jethro was glad someone was good in that position. Even though, when he was baptized into the church, he'd had to accept that, if so chosen, he would serve in the lifetime role of minister, it was a job he never wanted. As he'd shared with Susannah, his only security had been that the congregation knew how he spoke, and they didn't want to suffer through a note-less sermon from him any more than he did.

At the end of the lane, Jethro automatically turned Cocoa in the direction of Susannah's farm and let the horse pick its own pace up the hill. He hadn't seen her since they'd watched the *boppeli* together when Rachel and Ben had gone to the cider frolic last Saturday. He smiled at the memory. He'd longed to stop by on Visiting Sunday the next day. But since word was out about their relationship and she might not think it necessary to be in frequent contact, that had kept him away.

Jethro's lips twitched. He'd always been prompt about attending to his folks' needs, but the possibility of seeing Susannah had him rushing over now at his earliest opportunity. He rubbed a hand over his face, feeling the scar above his lip as his smile faded. When had it changed from liking to see Susannah to wanting to see her, to *needing* to see her? Not even to speak to, just to know she was near.

His heart rate, and his mood, picked up when he caught sight of Susannah. She was out in the orchard, picking up windfall apples. The rig had passed a few fence posts before Jethro reminded himself that his focus was to be sensitive to the sounds and motions of the buggy, not wondering whether the lovely apple picker would welcome an unexpected visit from him. Returning to his task, he directed the confused gelding to weave its way back and forth in their lane. Finally, he felt what his *daed* had noted. The buggy was pulling more to one side. But that wasn't all.

Tuning out the *clip-clop* of the gelding's hooves on the blacktop, Jethro narrowed his eyes in concentration. There it was. A peculiar rattling sounded from beneath his feet. Jethro estimated it to be somewhere near the front axle. When he eased the gelding into a trot, he felt a slight give in the buggy at the change of pace. He couldn't be certain of the exact issue until he got back to his folks' farm and climbed underneath, but at least it gave him some idea of what to address.

Guiding the gelding into Susannah's lane to turn the rig around, Jethro suppressed the urge to continue up the lane, park the rig and walk up to the orchard to help her. Picking up fallen apples with her would be much more interesting than staring at the undercarriage of his *daed's* buggy. But one was something he said he would do. The other…well, it was just what he wanted to. Jethro learned long ago not to expect to get what he wanted. With a final wistful glance toward the orchard, he checked for traffic before backing onto the road.

Now reluctant to waste any time fixing the buggy, he urged the gelding to a prompt pace. This time as the buggy surged forward, neither the rattling sound nor the give of the buggy beneath him was subtle. As they started down the hill, a sharp squeal followed by a pop startled the horse. Cocoa bolted, taking the shaft, all the way to the shaft eyes, away with him.

The fleeing reins whipped through Jethro's startled hands. He snatched at them, securing the tail end of the leather, only to be jerked almost to the dash for his efforts. The buggy—with no horse attached—was racing down the hill. Realizing the gelding would be better off away from the runaway rig, Jethro released the reins. Frightened by the bouncing shaft behind him, the horse raced away. An occasional spark flew up as hardware on the apparatus skidded along the blacktop.

Jethro shot a glance down the road. His

breath whistled out in relief. No one was approaching. The last thing he wanted was to crash into someone or to force them to drive into the ditch to evade him. He hoped Cocoa would be all right. At least the horse was outracing the buggy and wouldn't be part of the impending wreck.

The buggy hurtled down the hill at breakneck speed. Jethro rapidly debated his own escape. *I'm sorry,* Daed. *There're going to be a few more things to repair on your old rig.*

The buggy didn't have a storm front. The open area increased his avenues of escapes. But that way could be deadly. He'd do better jumping to the side. With a white-knuckled hand wrapped around the right front corner of the rig, Jethro considered the amber grass of the ditch that blurred by at increasing speed.

He glanced through the open front of the buggy in time to see the gelding swing safely into his folks' lane. Now for him. If the rig kept going straight, the road flattened out beyond the farmstead. The buggy would slow to a less frantic speed. But any bump or rock in the road could throw it off. And with traffic of steel-wheeled buggies and metal horse shoes, the surface was far from even.

It was the ditch then.

Jethro slid to the edge of the seat. Bracing

both hands on the sides of the door, he scanned the ditch ahead. No boulders loomed to hamper his fall. Snagging a ragged breath, Jethro launched himself through the door.

Chapter Ten

Ducking his head, Jethro attempted to roll on impact. Weed stems stabbed his face as he landed with a thud, his breath exiting in a whoosh. Bright stars whirled in his head as he lay momentarily motionless, waiting for the world to stop spinning. His mouth filled with the telltale metallic taste. Groaning, he rolled over and pressed a hand against the insistent throbbing in his head. *What happened to the buggy?* Pushing onto his knees, Jethro spat a bloody mouthful into the ditch before lurching to his feet. With help of the long stems of grass, he pulled himself out of the ditch.

The buggy had veered toward the left side of the road. Heading for the ditch, it'd hit the embankment of his folks' lane. The abrupt stop had flipped the buggy over and into the ditch on the far side. It lay on its top, one wheel obviously broken, the other three still spinning.

Swaying slightly as he surveyed the wreck, the blood drained from Jethro's face at the horrific thought of his parents taking that frantic ride. Neither of them was spry enough to have made the jump from the buggy. Then a flash of movement in the farmyard drew his attention. Expecting to see his horse, Jethro was bewildered to observe a young man rushing his scooter down the lane. When he looked in Jethro's direction, the youth's pale face was visible beneath his battered straw hat.

"Hey! Wait!" Jethro started a stumbling run in the boy's direction, the stiffness in his limbs slowing his pace. Without pausing, the youth darted out the far side of the lane. Jethro slowed to a rough jog and then a walk as the boy sped away down the road.

"Are you all right?" The frantic call came from behind him.

He looked back up the hill to see Susannah scrambling over the fence from the orchard before plunging down into the ditch. He waited while she clambered up the steep edge and hurried to his side. With a light hand on his shoulder, she scrutinized him from his missing hat to the mud ground into his pants and the toes of his boots.

"Your face is bleeding."

Jethro dabbed at his lip and other stinging spots on his cheek. He wasn't surprised when the tips of his fingers came away bright red. He furrowed his brow in pretend dismay. "Oh *nee*. D-do you think it will scar?"

What spared him a swat on his arm for the poor joke was most likely the concern that anywhere it landed would already hurt. An accurate assumption.

"Come to compare b-buggy wrecks?" He nodded with a rueful smile in the direction of the upturned vehicle.

Although she eyed him cautiously, Jethro was relieved when Susannah picked up that he wanted to make light of the situation. "Seems like an odd way to court a girl."

He found it even hurt to smile. "Maybe she's an odd girl."

"She is that, for sure and certain." Frowning, Susannah turned to consider the wreck. "I think we might need a warning sign on this road."

"Hmm." Wincing, Jethro rolled his shoulders experimentally before crossing his arms at his chest. "I think we need one on the b-boy instead. I'm p-pretty certain that was your former hired hand racing away on his scooter. I think he m-might have b-been in the b-barn when I came to work on the b-buggy."

Staring down the road in the direction of the vanishing youth, Susannah sighed as she twisted her hands together. "Do you think the accident was intentional?"

"*Ja.* I know enough about b-buggies t-to know what just happened d-doesn't easily d-do so. Not without help." The admission was hard. And concerning.

Susannah folded her arms as well. "I thought the reason he was sabotaging my place was because he was unhappy with something I told him to do. Or the lectures I gave him when he seemed to be willfully trying me. But that wouldn't be the case with what happened today." She contemplated the wrecked buggy. "Were you the intended target? Or the bishop?" she murmured.

Jethro shook his head, stilling abruptly when it throbbed in protest. "I hardly know the b-boy. I d-don't know why he'd t-target m-me."

"If not you, then the bishop. But why?"

His troubled gaze shifted from the wreck to the farmyard. "I d-don't have an answer t-to that right now. But what I d-do know is that I need to find m-my horse." He started for the lane, gritting his teeth against aches that loudly objected to his determined stride.

Susannah walked by his side. The gelding hadn't gone far. Shaking and lathered, it stood next to Jethro's buggy. Jethro talked soothingly as he freed the horse from the broken shaft before running a careful hand down its legs. "Ready t-to go back to our house b-boy? T-too m-much excitement for you here?"

"Is he all right?"

"Looks that way." Jethro sighed heavily as he stroked the horse's sweaty neck. "I'm so glad."

"You want to leave him here and drive one of my horses?"

What he wanted to do was wrap his arms around her and just hold her a moment. Just to absorb her warmth, practicality and support. Just to take a moment to appreciate the fact, although he was sore and knew he'd be stiff later, that it wasn't worse. Just to dwell a bit in the possibility of a future with this woman. Instead, he ran a final hand down the gelding's slick neck.

"We'll see how he is after taking a look at the b-buggy. If he's sore or skittish at all, I m-might t-take you up on that."

A quick search in the barn revealed a bag of horse treats. He gave Cocoa a few before leaving him inside with the other horse for company. Then he headed to the wreck at the end of the lane.

Jethro longed to take hold of Susannah's hand as they studied what had been an old but still usable buggy. Along with the broken wheel, the buggy's front end was crumpled. The axle was bent. He could see the impact from the flip over the lane had caused one wall to separate from the roof of the buggy. There would be no repairing it. Jethro trembled again at the thought of his parents as passengers during the wild ride instead of himself. He exhaled shakily. "I guess I owe my *daed* a new rig."

"I'd say he owes you his life," Susannah countered quietly. "No guarantee it wouldn't have happened to him on the hill with the same results to the buggy and..." Her voice faded away.

She didn't have to say it. Jethro already knew. And much worse results for his folks.

Later that afternoon, as he and Bishop Weaver stood at the end of the lane, absorbing the scattered debris, Jethro was almost tempted to wrap his arms around his *daed* in a tight embrace. The moment the impulse arose, he suppressed it. His *daed* would be shocked and annoyed by the display of affection. Jethro had learned that years ago at the age of six when his father had been gone for a week, having traveled to Ohio for a gathering of church leadership.

Thrilled to see his *daed* after spending a week being alternatively ignored or chastised by his mother, Jethro had run to him as soon as the bishop had climbed off the bus with a gathering of other Amish men. Throwing his arms around his *daed's* lean waist, Jethro had hugged him, his more approachable parent, with all his strength. A gruff, "Stop that, boy," had been followed by a grip prying his stick-thin arms from his father's torso. Hanging his head, Jethro had shuffled to the side as the bishop said his farewells to the men he'd traveled with and greeted his wife and younger son. Jethro had never attempted to hug either of his parents again.

"I'll confirm what caused it after I get it p-pulled out. From the way the whole shaft came away, it had t-to b-be intentional. I saw the Schlabach b-boy racing from the farm on his scooter. Susannah has had some issues with him earlier." Jethro stroked his beard as he turned to his father. "Any reason he m-might t-turn his attention t-to you as well and wreck your b-buggy?"

The bishop's mouth compressed into a lipless line as he studied the carcass of the buggy. But Jethro had an impression the wreck wasn't what the man was seeing. With a shrug, he pivoted to retrieve the team of Belgians he'd brought over to pull the damaged rig out. At his father's abrupt, "Wait!" he paused. Expecting to hear a comment about the Schlabach boy or even the damaged buggy, Jethro stiffened at the bishop's choice of topic.

"You need to stop seeing Susannah Mast."

"What?" Jethro cocked his head, unsure that he'd heard right. For sure and certain, he'd been expecting the subject to come up at some point. He'd even made himself scarce just to evade the conversation. But he hardly expected it to be now, when there seemed other much more pressing issues for the bishop than directing his adult son's private life.

"She will wreck your life, surely as this buggy is wrecked."

Jethro turned around to face his father. "Susannah is a *gut* woman."

"*Ja.* But not for you. You need someone who can give you children. A family. Susannah can't do that. She is better matched with an older man who wouldn't be looking for that in a wife. You'd do better to look to her daughter. She's not that much younger than you. You could build a life, a large family, with her."

"I know what I need." Jethro hardly recognized his voice as he ground out the words. He liked Rebecca. She was a sweet girl. But the thought of courting her instead of Susannah coated the back of his throat with bile.

"You need to obey your parents. Honor your father and mother, as is commanded."

Jethro easily identified the biblical verses. Ones that'd been drummed into him since before he could remember. At this moment, they stabbed at him. He'd strived to obey his folks all his life, even at the price of his own happiness. It'd been worth the cost, for he did honor his parents. But what he was feeling for Susannah was not wrong. It gave him a spark of contentment—happiness—he hadn't felt in a long, long time, if ever. It was something worth fighting for. Still, his stomach clenched and sweat beaded on his forehead as he countered his father.

"I've d-done that all m-my life." The headache that'd never fully dissipated since his dive into the ditch throbbed anew. "As b-bishop, you'll be glad to hear that I know scripture as well. What about 'fathers, p-provoke not your children to wrath'? I've already m-married a wife you've chosen for me. My b-brother's. I would've stayed married to Louisa. B-built a life with her. B-but it wasn't *Gott's* will. This t-time I will m-marry whom *I* choose."

"It isn't *Gott's* will that you marry Susannah."

Jethro walked over to the waiting team of Belgians. The large heads of the normally placid geldings were lifted, eyes rounded and chestnut ears pricked forward at the raised voices. Drawing in a ragged breath, Jethro concentrated on monitoring his tone as he walked the team past the bishop on his way down into the ditch. "Isn't His? Or isn't *yours*?"

Conscious of his father's gaze on him, Jethro focused on safely hitching the Belgians to a section of the broken buggy. His hands were shaking so badly, it took him three tries to attach the now wheel-less shell of the buggy to the team. With a quiet command, the geldings lunged into their collars to pull their load out of the ditch and into the bishop's yard. Briskly unhooking that piece, Jethro returned for another, relieved to see that his *daed* had gone into the house.

He wished he could sort out the wreckage of his emotions as quickly as the debris scattered in the ditch. He didn't like conflict. That didn't mean he couldn't face it when necessary, but doing so troubled him. Greatly. Jethro snorted as he urged the Belgians up the lane with the second load. One more reason why he hoped never to be a minister who might have to address a misbehaving flock.

But on this, he wasn't misbehaving. As he'd told his *daed*, Susannah was a *gut* woman. A woman any man would be happy to have as a wife. Wasn't his father urging other men to court her? Why not him? Surely it wasn't wrong to want to marry the woman of your choice. And Susannah was everything he wanted.

Securing the geldings, Jethro returned to the ditch to collect smaller pieces, ones he didn't need the team for, from the wreck. He wanted this courtship to be real. He wanted Susannah as his wife. But that wasn't the arrangement they'd agreed to. Susannah had given him no hint that she wanted anything else than a brief reprieve from other suitors. Unwanted suitors.

Gathering the last few pieces he could find in the tall grass, Jethro gazed across the field to Susannah's farm. Oh, how he longed to be considered as a serious suitor by this woman. Because what he was feeling for her was anything but temporary.

Chapter Eleven

There were already a dozen rigs in the farmyard the following day when Susannah secured Nutmeg to the rail. Upon gathering the cleaning supplies she'd brought from the buggy, she waved a greeting to the woman she spied on the porch industriously applying her broom. Her good friend, Willa Lapp, paused in her sweeping as Susannah came up the stairs.

"Do you think I can convince them to plan a frolic to help me clean my house?" Susannah jested.

"Maybe if you're preparing for a church service or a wedding. I'll make the suggestion that they do yours...right after they do mine." Willa smiled as she eyed Susannah's assortment of rags and bottles. "They're going to give you a hard time about not bringing food."

Susannah grinned in response, knowing

what was coming. "They'd give me a harder time if I had."

With a sympathetic nod, Willa put the broom in motion again. "*Ach*, that's for sure and certain."

Opening the door, Susannah found several other women bustling around the roomy kitchen. Bumping the door with her hip to close it, she stayed just inside, out of the flow of traffic, as she responded to the chorused greetings. "Where do you want me?"

"Not in here, that's for sure," quipped a gray-haired woman near the stove. Laughter circled the room.

Susannah heaved a wounded sigh. "I'll remember that, Waneta Gingerich. And next time you host church, I'll bring several desserts and make sure to transfer them to your dishes and serve them up saying 'Waneta made this.'"

"Anyone who knows us wouldn't make that mistake," came the prompt retort, followed by more chuckles.

"Actually, I had a cookie or two of yours at the cider frolic that weren't bad at all. I thought they were safe when I saw Rachel bring them in. When I complimented her on them and she said they were yours, you could've knocked me over with a feather. And not because I was sick from them, either." Mary Raber, Rachel's mother-in-law, winked from the doorway.

"I've been working on my skills," Susannah said, tamping down her unexpected delight at the comment. "I'll just have to keep sneaking them in somehow so I can prove it to all you doubters in the district."

"I don't know. According to Naomi, you have a whole new set of skills." Ruth Schrock, the wife of the owner of the furniture business in town and Ben's boss, raised her eyebrows from where she'd just handed her young daughter to one of the preteen girls who'd watch the smaller children while their mothers cleaned.

Susannah, along with the rest, turned to look at the older woman who was currently doing dishes. Naomi's cheeks grew rosy as she turned away from the sink. "*Ja*. The reason Leroy Albrecht is courting me now is because of Susannah's skills as a matchmaker."

Susannah's eyes weren't the only ones that widened at the news. A quick review of the kitchen revealed many speculative glances now aimed her way. Susannah stifled a snort at the attention. Single women, both widows and those who'd never married, as well as mothers with many daughters who were perennially in search of something that might help their children find a spouse, were eyeing her with consideration. Content to remain a widow, Susannah was in the minority in the community.

Her desire to smirk quickly faded as she acknowledged many were not smiling. Marriage was a matter of economics, companionship and a foundation for children. Just because her marriage had primarily been of the former and latter didn't mean that others didn't long for those as well, in addition to the allure of companionship. Her attitude wasn't entirely fair to her husband, Vernon. They'd developed a comfortable companionship over the years. Just not—her heart gave a couple distinct thuds at the abrupt realization—companionship like she'd been relishing lately with Jethro.

Uncomfortable with the direction of her thoughts and the attention aimed her way, Susannah lifted the supplies in her hands. "Since I won't be in the kitchen, where do you want me to start?"

Although they were preparing the farmhouse for Hannah Bartel—she and her husband Gabe were moving from the small apartment they'd been living in over the quilt shop in town—Waneta was in charge of the day's cleaning frolic. Wiping her hands on her apron, the gray-haired woman stepped forward. "I don't think anyone has been upstairs yet. Would you mind starting up there? We'll send others up as soon as possible."

"*Ja.* Sounds *gut,*" Susannah hastened to assure her. Sounded very good in fact, as it might forestall any curious questions arising from Naomi's announcement. With a smiling nod for those in the kitchen and others she passed working in the main-floor rooms, Susannah opened the door to the narrow stairway, trotted up the steps and stepped into the first bedroom.

The old farmhouse had been empty for a year or so following the passing of its *Englisch* owners. Although smaller than many houses built by the Amish, it still had two bedrooms upstairs and a small bath. Sturdy, it would be a nice place for Hannah and Gabe, the local EMS provider. According to their district's rules, new Amish owners had a year to convert an *Englisch* home to Plain standards. Susannah wondered how many of those who'd purchased homes waited until the eleventh month before leaving the power grid.

She wasn't sure what Hannah and Gabe's plans were. Gabe was Mennonite. In order to marry him, Hannah hadn't been baptized into the church and so wasn't subject to the rules of the *Ordnung.* Even so, the couple, widely accepted in the Plain community, tried to abide by the lifestyle Hannah had grown up in.

Susannah studied the empty room. At least there was no carpet here to pull up. As Amish didn't use electricity, which meant no vacuums, carpets were difficult to keep clean. Most of the floors in the district were wood like this or covered with linoleum with some woven rugs here and there to provide warmth and color. Susannah had dragged her share of rugs outside to beat the dust out over the years.

Setting her cleaning supplies on the floor, Susannah rolled up her sleeves. The house was much more spacious than the couple's current apartment where they'd resided for the past year. It would be exciting for them to move into a new home, something Susannah had never done. As the youngest daughter in a family with no sons, she'd inherited the farm when her folks had died, her father passing when she was in her teens. Susannah knew her husband had considered the farm more appealing than any personal attributes she might have had. Her and Vernon's youthful marriage had been based on expediency; she'd needed help on the farm and he'd needed an occupation, although farming wouldn't have been his first choice. And it'd showed.

To shed the melancholy thoughts, Susannah

grabbed some supplies and headed into the bathroom. The little room filled with the sharp smell of vinegar as she poured it, along with a sufficient amount of water, into the bucket.

Returning to the bedroom, Susannah frowned at the shadows in the room. Although every square inch of the room would be scrubbed, the dim lighting made it difficult to see. If it were up to her, she'd immediately repaint the room in a brighter color. In the meantime, she narrowed her eyes at the small white rectangle by the doorframe and drummed her fingers against her leg. Had they been working in natural light downstairs, or was the electricity still on in the house? And were those working today using it? There was one way to find out.

Striding to the door, she put her thumb under the switch and pushed upward. With a soft click, the room brightened, making the problem areas much easier to see. *Gut!* Now if only she was left alone to work, the fact that she was using it up here wouldn't be known.

Even as the thought crossed her mind, the door to the stairway creaked open, followed by the hesitant tread announcing someone was coming up the steps. Scowling, Susannah clicked off the light. Selecting a large rag, she dipped it into the vinegar solution and began wiping down the walls. She was halfway across the first one when, at a sound at the door, she turned to see Emma Beiler poking her head into the room.

"How's it going up here?" the petite woman asked.

"Pretty well. Not a large room, so it shouldn't take too long."

"Do you want some help?" Emma stepped through the door.

"*Denki.* That would be appreciated. Would you mind starting on the opposite side?"

"Sure." Snagging a rag, Emma dipped it into the bucket and began scrubbing the far wall. The two worked in silence for a while before Susannah heard the other woman clear her throat.

"You know...what Naomi said in the kitchen got me thinking..."

Susannah blinked at the smudge on the wall before her. *"Ja?"* she responded as she re-wet the rag and went back to work. Absently scrubbing at the dark spot, her attention was focused on the woman across the room. Emma and her twin sister Elizabeth had never been married. Perhaps five years or so older than Susannah, Emma produced the straw hats many in the community had worn for as long as Susannah could remember, running the business out of the sisters' little house. Always thinking of

Emma and her twin as a unit, Susannah had never thought of one of them as wanting a marriage of her own. She frowned at the stubborn smudge. Which had been foolishness on her part.

Their culture placed such importance on marriage; there was unfortunately a stigma on being older and single. If it was uncomfortable enough for a woman, it was even tougher for a bachelor. Unmarried men were less common than unmarried females because if either sex were to leave the Amish life, it was more likely the men. Beyond the advantage of numbers, because the men did the proposing in their society, it was assumed if an older man was single, he either couldn't get anyone or he was too particular. Dubbed an "old boy," it wasn't a flattering term.

"I was wondering… If you wouldn't mind… If you could think of someone who might be interested…"

Feeling for the woman, Susannah turned to face Emma's tentative expression. "Getting Naomi and Leroy together was more of an accident than anything else. But if I can, I'd be happy to send someone in your direction." Her heart clenched at the hope in the other woman's face. "Did you have anyone in mind?" she added lamely.

"*Nee.*" It was said with a sigh. "But I haven't thought about it for a long while."

Susannah bit her lip at the obvious wistfulness. "Are there any particular traits you might be looking for?"

"Breathing?" Emma smiled before cocking her head and considering the ceiling for a moment. "And kind."

"I'll keep those in mind." That and more for the obviously lonely woman. But there was one thing Susannah wanted the woman to be certain of before she assumed a role she wasn't looking for and wasn't sure she was capable of. "Although I might not find anyone."

"I know that. But then again…you might."

They worked further in silence. When she'd completed wiping down the walls on her side of the room, Emma set her rag with the rest of the supplies. "I need to get back downstairs and finish the task I was working on before… our talk. *Denki* again."

"Thank you for your help. Oh, would you send someone up with a dry mop or broom I can throw a rag over to wipe down the ceiling?"

"I'll let someone know as soon as I get downstairs."

A short time later, the door creaked open again followed by footsteps on the stairs. Susannah turned as someone entered, carrying not one mop, but two. She relaxed at the sight of Linda Esh. There'd be no request for a matchmaker here. Linda was already a wife and mother of a large family.

"Emma said you needed this?"

Taking one mop, Susannah leaned the other against the wall. *"Ja. Denki."* When Linda didn't retreat back down the stairs, Susannah shrugged. Draping a large rag over the mop, she started systematically wiping it over the ceiling, clearing it of an occasional cobweb.

The odor of vinegar was strengthened when Linda returned to the room with a fresh bucket of solution. Fishing out another old cloth diaper Susannah had brought as rags, the woman dampened it and began cleaning the windows. Susannah was halfway across the ceiling when the woman cleared her throat.

"About what Naomi said downstairs… My oldest *dochder* seems to be overlooked by the young men in the district and I was wondering…"

Susannah's brisk motions across the ceiling slowed as her brows rose.

"I've heard that the bishop thinks it's time his son marries again. Jethro's quiet, but he's a *gut* man. He'd be quite a catch."

Susannah froze at the woman's words.

She stared at the ceiling where her mop was pressed, the edges of the rag dangling down. Her emotions were suddenly as frayed as the edges of the old cloth. Apparently she and Jethro hadn't been doing such a good job in presenting themselves as a courting couple. Either that or the woman was intentionally ignoring the news, knowing as Susannah did that the notion of the two of them together was foolish.

It wasn't surprising someone thought of Jethro as a prospective husband. The bishop's frequent pushing of his son toward courtship was Jethro's reason for entering into their agreement in the first place. But still, to hear it voiced aloud? Susannah felt like she'd unwittingly swallowed the vinegar solution and her stomach was now rebelling. In the silence behind her, she knew she needed to say something. But the thought that someone was particularly interested in Jethro, *her* Jethro… Lowering the mop handle, Susannah rubbed her uneasy midsection.

Fortunately, the other woman filled the quiet when she moved to the next window. "There's also the older Raber boy, who just came back from the *Englisch*. But you'd always worry that he might leave again. Besides, Aaron always seemed a bit wild. Or maybe the youngest Schrock *bruder*, Gideon? His older *brieder* seem to be doing all right. Anyone can see the Schrocks are fine-looking and responsible men."

Susannah silently blew out a breath as the discussion moved away from Jethro. She couldn't blame the woman. As a mother, you always hoped for your children to make a good match. She wanted the same for Rebecca, who was Linda's oldest daughter's age.

"I will keep your comments in mind. But you need to know that what happened with Naomi and Leroy was just…"

The second and final window complete, Linda set her rag next to the bucket. Her smile was lopsided, her cheeks slightly pink with what could be exertion from cleaning or embarrassment. Susannah knew which it would be for her. "I understand. But I wanted to ask before others did."

Susannah nodded numbly as the woman exited the room. Spotting the extra mop, she almost called the woman to take it back downstairs. The last thing she wanted after the two previous helpers was more company. Quickly finishing the ceiling, she prepared to mop the floor. And cringed when she heard the door creak at the bottom of the stairs.

That was the way it went for the rest of the morning. When one woman went down, another was soon mounting the stairs. Even though Susannah began to direct them to a room she wasn't working in for a task, new helpers at some point poked their head into where she was and brought up her unexpected and unwanted role as a matchmaker.

Susannah tried to guide the conversations to the upcoming election for minister. All acknowledged that it was an honorable role to serve *Gott* in such a way, although many admitted few wanted to be chosen for the lifelong, unpaid position. And then they worked the discussion around to what they'd be interested in as a match for themselves. Or their children. Or their sisters. Even their grandchildren.

Susannah didn't know whether to clean faster to avoid any more private moments with those seeking her questionable matrimonial skills or to take her time in case it would be worse downstairs among the others. Although appreciative of the revolving help, she was thrilled for a few moments' respite when there were no new footsteps on the stairs.

Shaking her head, she scoured the sink in the small bathroom. *I'll probably hear the door's creak in my dreams. What have I gotten myself into?* The idea had been amusing at first—connecting Leroy, her unwanted suitor who wanted someone talented in the kitchen, with Naomi, who was proud of the fact that she was. But it wasn't so amusing any more.

With an ear tuned for any noise from the door, Susannah replayed some of the conversations as she rinsed the sink. *Well, now I know what the single women in the district want in a husband.* Furrowing her brow, she polished the faucet handles. *If I were talking to a matchmaker*—she rolled her eyes at the notion of herself in the role—*what would I look for in one?* Jethro had asked her that once. Originally mocking the question, she'd later struggled to answer it. The discussion had been gnawing at her at odd moments ever since.

If and when she had to marry, Susannah was going to make sure it was someone she wanted. She'd make a list of qualities, much like what she looked for in a buck when matching with her does. If you wanted specific characteristics, you needed to identify and look for them, especially when you were working with a small herd. Her lips twitched. Or community. Otherwise you got what you got.

If she remarried, she didn't expect a love match. She hoped for a good working relationship and help with the farm. A hardworking man. Patient around livestock. She smiled as she recalled Jethro's comment about his draft team going courting for him. Mechanically inclined would be helpful as well.

Susannah paused while shifting her attention to the tub. It would also be pleasant to have someone she enjoyed being around. Today, Emma had requested a kind man. That was certainly an attractive quality. The other traits women had mentioned—a good sense of humor, fun, able to laugh but serious when necessary, someone who listened—Susannah could agree with.

She bent over the tub. *Jethro is hardworking. He's good with livestock. He can fix anything. He's...* Sitting back on her heels, Susannah stared unseeing at the beige tile above the white tub. Jethro had all the qualities she looked for in a husband. It was almost as if she'd been describing him. *Oh dear. And when had he become my Jethro? That wasn't our agreement at all.* Theirs was only to be a fake relationship. He wouldn't appreciate her getting other ideas.

This time when the squeak of the door interrupted her thoughts, she was relieved. Hannah Bartel stopped in the doorway. A contented wife of less than a year, Hannah wouldn't be looking for a match for herself, she had no single sisters that needed a union, and no marriage-age children. This should be a safe conversation.

Hannah inhaled with appreciative slowness as she surveyed the bathroom. "It smells clean in here. Looks like you're finishing up. My timing is *gut* as I've been instructed to tell you that lunch is ready."

"Sounds *wunderbar*." Gathering her supplies, Susannah looked up to find Hannah studying her.

"So…you and Jethro, huh?"

Susannah's hand tightened on the handle of her bucket. She didn't respond. Couldn't respond. Despite her and Jethro's agreement, following the unexpected emotional turmoil of the morning, she hesitated to mislead this woman.

Hannah wore a sweet smile. "I'm glad. He's a *gut* man. He deserves happiness. Take care of him. I know you'll be *gut* to him."

Would she? Susannah wasn't so sure, now that she was aware of other women—more suitable than her—who were interested in Jethro. Maybe the best thing she could do for him was to free him from their fake relationship so he could pursue a real one. She swallowed against the lump in her throat as she followed Hannah downstairs. Why did the thought make her feel as empty as the vacant rooms she'd just cleaned?

Chapter Twelve

Susannah drew Nutmeg to a halt, wondering if she was making a mistake in stopping here on her way home from the cleaning frolic. At least she knew Lavinia Schlabach was home. John's *mamm* was hanging clothes on the line. She stepped out from between the sheets that billowed in the breeze to see who had driven up her lane. Susannah remained on the buggy seat, unsure of how to proceed. She'd known Lavinia for years, liked and respected the woman, but they weren't close friends. How did one accuse a woman's son of potentially dangerous activities without offending her? And that, on top of having fired the youth the previous week, probably removing a needed income source for the family.

Still, while what John had done to her had been nuisances—although she didn't put hurting Nutmeg in that category—they hadn't been potentially deadly like the situation with the bishop's buggy. What had caused the sullen boy's normally harmless actions to take a more dangerous turn?

When Lavinia shaded her eyes in an effort to identify who had arrived, Susannah knew she couldn't delay longer. Fastening her jacket against an inner chill as much as the drop in October temperature, she climbed down from the buggy and started across the shaggy yard. The laundry on the line attested to the financial challenges Lavinia had endured. The sheets flapping in the light wind were worn and bore patches, as did the socks that spun on the small, circular rack hanging from the main clothesline. Still, the dress of the woman standing among these, although worn as well, was neat and clean, as was her lean figure.

Susannah sighed after a quick scan of the laundry. No pants or shirts hung with the other items flapping in the breeze. John was Lavinia's youngest child and the only one living at home. John wasn't here. If he was, his clothes surely would've been on the line. Still, even if he wasn't living at home, his mother might know where he was.

"Hello, Lavinia." Susannah stopped a few feet from the clothesline.

"Susannah." There were a few beats of silence while Lavinia studied her before continuing. "I know why you're here. I don't know where he is. I haven't seen him since the day he came home early from your place."

"I'm so sorry I had to let him go. I don't know what he mentioned, but he'd intentionally hurt my mare. I couldn't allow that."

Sighing, Lavinia dropped her head. "It's all right. I understand. He'd been sorely troubled since he heard of his father's passing."

"I'm sorry about that as well."

"You needn't be. It was *Gott's* will. Mervin left the Amish...and me, over ten years ago. I shouldn't say it, as he was my husband, but they've been a better ten years than the ones that came before. I appreciate all the district has done for me, both before he left and after. I don't know what I would've done without their intervention and support." Her prematurely lined face lifted in a rueful smile. "Including the money that's been provided over the past decade."

"We take care of each other. That's as it should be." Figuring it might make it easier for the woman to talk if they weren't facing each other like unintentional adversaries, Susannah grabbed an item from the nearby basket and a handful of clothespins and hung it on the line. A moment later, Lavinia did the same.

"John saw some things he shouldn't have. He experienced some things he shouldn't have, either. The older ones were bigger and quicker to get out of the way. I tried to protect him as much as I could, but I was dealing with the same thing. Still, John took it very hard when Mervin was…" The woman's voice drifted off as she bent to the basket and hung up a few more items.

Susannah stayed silent as well, letting Lavinia determine what she wanted to share. Many things had been attempted to impact Mervin Schlabach's behavior—visits by the ministers, the *Englisch* jail, shunning—until the man had left the community for an unsettled life among the *Englisch*.

"Before he went, Mervin was always talking poorly about the ministers. Bishop Weaver, David Petersheim and your husband. I think John blames them for what happened."

Susannah's fingers tightened on the clothespin as she hung a ragged towel. The information was enlightening and disturbing. She and the Weavers had been targeted. David Petersheim had passed away a few years ago and his family had moved out of the area. And therefore, apparently, out of the troubled boy's reach? "Doesn't John know when someone is excommunicated from the church, the district must be unanimous in the decision?"

"That's not what he'd heard from his father before he left. It was never Mervin's fault. Not surprising when he never showed remorse. I'm afraid he poisoned the boy's thinking. Mervin would fly off the handle at everything. I suppose I wasn't surprised, but it was still painful when John started stealing. When I'd confront him on it, it was like he was anticipating it." Lavinia shook her head sadly as she asked quietly, "Did he steal from you?"

"Not that I know of."

"I'm glad of that at least. John never had a *gut* role model. At least when the older children were little, my folks lived in the connected *daadi haus* and had some influence. They passed when John was an infant, so after that it was just... Mervin."

Susannah nodded solemnly, knowing remarriage hadn't been possible for Lavinia. Even though the man had left her, she could never divorce him, as they would always be married in the eyes of the church.

"But we always managed, with the help of the community." Having hung the last item in the basket, Lavinia crossed her arms over her narrow chest and stared toward the road.

"I worry for John. I don't know where he's staying. Folks tell me when they catch sight of him. I've heard some folks have been missing eggs and such. I just want him home and safe." Sighing, she picked up the empty basket. "Wish I could tell him that he's striking out at the wrong folks. The only one to blame was his *daed*. But he doesn't want to hear it." When she turned her gaze to her visitor, its bleakness cut straight through Susannah's heart. She couldn't imagine not knowing Amos's whereabouts, and that he needed help wherever he was. There were no limits to a mother's love.

"Would you like some *kaffi*?" The suggestion was tentative.

"Denki." Susannah recognized it as more a plea to talk than anything else. Even with the many things waiting for her at home, it was an offer Susannah couldn't and wouldn't turn down. "That would be *gut*." She followed Lavinia into the house.

The muffled chatter made Susannah smile. Leaning on the smooth branch of the apple tree, she watched Jethro, Rebecca and Amos picking apples from a tree several yards away. The air was crisp with the scent of the ripe fruit, the faint hum of insects and a nippy reminder of cooler weather to come. The descending sun cast a relative glow over the orchard. Susannah's smile slipped as she inhaled sharply. The day seemed brighter when Jethro was around. At least Rebecca and Amos seemed to think so. They'd been thrilled when Jethro had happened by while they were using some time before chores to harvest the fruit. Susannah had been as well. But she wasn't going to show it. Particularly after the cleaning frolic yesterday.

She should really stop this farce. Jethro didn't need her help anymore. Based on what she'd heard yesterday from some women in the district, he wouldn't even need to go courting. Several interested parties would find a way to make a trail to his door.

As for her reason for the fake courtship, Jethro had brought his team over yesterday while she'd been gone and completed a large share of the field work. Now, with just a few big days in the field, she and Amos should be able to complete the rest of the work. Since finishing it before colder weather arrived had been her stated purpose for evading unwanted suitors, the motivation no longer existed.

But had that really been her reason? Susannah acknowledged her real motivation had been that she didn't care for any of her potential suitors like she now cared for Jethro. She rubbed a hand over her forehead. How could she tell him that she wanted to make their pretend courtship real? He'd be embarrassed to hear his former babysitter confess she wanted to be his…what? His wife? Envisioning the awkward admission, and equally embarrassing rejection, Susannah turned as red as the surrounding apples.

She'd been the one to insist that whatever happened, they stay friends. But it was too small of a community for that. It would be painful enough to continue to see him with whomever he'd eventually choose as his wife and their growing family over the years.

Sniffling, Susannah brushed the back of her hand against the faint prickling in her nose. Her head lifted at the sound of Rebecca's laughter. At the other tree, she watched her daughter grin as she caught an apple dropped by Jethro, who'd climbed up the tree's trunk to reach some of the higher branches. Susannah's breath caught as he smiled in return from his precarious perch.

Her stomach twisted at the sight. Jethro had been more quiet than usual lately. What if he was already losing interest in her and turning his interest elsewhere? To someone whom he'd also been around lately who was pretty and charming—and much more appropriate for him? What if she had to watch Jethro court, marry and raise a family with her own daughter? It made sense. Closer in age, Rebecca could give him a family. What if in the future Susannah would babysit her grandchildren—his children—the ones she couldn't give him?

Susannah's face contorted briefly at the image of having the man she cared for as a son-in-law. When Jethro looked up and caught her gaze, she ducked her head. Pivoting, she grabbed at the first apple she saw. Jethro would be a *wunderbar* husband for Rebecca. As a mother, Susannah couldn't ask for a better partner for her daughter. But she didn't know if she could bear it. And for that reason, she needed to break off their fake engagement and point him in the direction of other women in the community. At the thought of losing their cherished connection, her hand clenched around the apple, denting the fruit.

"Are you all right?"

Jethro raised his eyebrows when Susannah flinched at his words. Surely his father hadn't had the same distasteful lecture with her that he'd had with him? That was more his mother's tactic than his father's. But that was entirely possible, too. He longed to touch Susannah on her shoulder, to gently prompt her to face him, but he didn't really have the right to do so. Yet. Although she'd smiled when he'd arrived, Susannah hadn't said much, which in itself was odd. Instead of staying by her as he'd wanted to when he'd found them in the orchard, he'd allowed himself to be drawn away by Rebecca and Amos. But when their eyes met and she'd seemed distraught, it would've taken a six-horse draft hitch to keep him away.

Finally, her shoulders straightened and she turned to face him. "*Ja.* Certainly." Her voice was as peculiar as the smile it accompanied. It definitely didn't emanate from her eyes as it normally did. Her eyes weren't smiling at all. They were troubled.

Jethro took a step closer.

Breaking his gaze, Susannah bent to put an apple in the basket at her feet. "I wanted to thank you for your help yesterday."

He'd come over, hoping to see her. After the conversation with his father, he'd wanted to be with her. To replace the uneasiness he'd felt with the joy that always filled him when he was near Susannah. They'd covered many more acres than he'd expected, but his draft team had been tired by the time he'd finally given up and left when she'd never come home.

Because she seemed uncomfortable facing

him, he plucked a few nearby apples and set them in the basket. "Glad t-to d-do it. It was p-part of our arrangement."

He frowned when her face paled to a color more closely matched to the *kapp* she wore than her normally tanned cheeks. She moved to another branch. One farther from him. There were still plenty of reachable apples on the one she'd left. "Speaking of that. Your name came up at the cleaning frolic at Hannah Bartel's yesterday. More than once." Susannah tossed a smile over her shoulder that was more dismal than the one she'd offered him before.

Other than their fake relationship, which he'd gladly have folks talk about, Jethro wasn't fond of being a topic of discussion. Had his mother gotten to Susannah? From where he'd been working, he could see her rig had been home all day yesterday. Had she gotten a ride to the gathering?

"About our courtship?"

"*Nee.* Apparently we need to do a better job of that. Or perhaps—" she cleared her throat "—we should end it. Because these were women who would like you to be courting them or their daughters." The small branch bowed before springing up again with the force of which she'd tugged the fruit from the tree.

Jethro's stomach dropped. He scowled as he reached for a pair of apples. With a grunt, he briskly snapped them off at the stem. The last thing he wanted to do was end their courtship. As for there being women in the district who wanted him to come calling? That was certainly a surprise. But useless information. He didn't want to even think about courting someone else. He was much more interested in figuring out a way to have the woman whom he was pretend courting want to make it real.

And from what Susannah was saying, he was doing a pretty poor job of even faking a relationship. More evidence of why he should avoid courting in general. Sweat beaded on his forehead as he jerked a few more apples from the branches.

"Don't you want to know who they were? Aren't you even slightly curious?"

"Nee." He pulled down another couple handfuls of apples. "If we're supposed t-to b-be courting, why are they asking you about wanting to walk out with m-me?" Jethro glared at the fruit in his hand before he put it in the basket. He could see his *daed's* hand in this somehow. His folks knew a direct approach didn't always work with him. He wasn't surprised they'd try another method to break up

what they presumed to be an inappropriate relationship of his.

When Susannah didn't respond from where she worked on the other side of the tree, Jethro darted a frowning glance in her direction. Was she trying to push him off on other women? A blemish on the apple in his hand caught his eye. Well, that was something he could certainly relate to. Cocking his arm, Jethro pitched it far into the connecting field and watched it bounce hard before rolling into the grass. Susannah couldn't possibly be caring for him, as he was her, if she was that eager to get rid of him.

"Apparently I've gained a reputation as something of a matchmaker. That's why they were asking me. Naomi and Leroy are now seeing each other after my 'baking lesson.' She announced that I was the one that brought them together. I was working upstairs. It was a regular parade of women who came up to see me after that. Some wanting someone to court them. Some wanting a match for their daughters. A few of the single men in the area were specifically mentioned. One of them was you."

Putting a trio of apples in her basket, she turned to him and mused ruefully, "Maybe my skills at cooking up something weren't meant to be in the kitchen. Maybe I'm better at blending people together instead of ingredients."

The tension in Jethro's shoulders relaxed. Perhaps she wasn't trying to get rid of him, after all. "B-be careful. There m-might still be m-mishaps waiting to happen. My favorite is the fork you baked into the corn bread."

Plucking an apple from the tree, Susannah threw it at him. Catching it one-handed, Jethro contentedly sighed at this more Susannah-like action as he looked it over. Rubbing it on his sleeve, he took a bite.

"The goats had made a commotion outside. I ran over to the window to make sure they were all right, which they fortunately were, and when I got back, I'd forgotten that I'd propped the fork on the edge of the bowl. It slid into the batter when I wasn't looking."

Jethro took another bite from the apple. Now that Susannah seemed closer to normal, he was comfortable enough to ask, "So, was there anything that m-made you think of cooking up something else for m-me?"

Grimacing, Susannah twisted her hands together as she looked away. "Actually, it was a little bit disturbing to have someone ask about seeing the man that I'm supposedly seeing."

It was like the sun coming out, the way her words warmed his heart. Jethro wanted to embrace the apple tree beside him. Embrace Susannah. He pitched the apple core into the field, much more gently this time. "As you say, we need to do a better job with our own courtship. How would you like to go to the auction with me tomorrow?"

She went still at his words. Above the simple neckline of her dress, her slender throat bobbed in a hard swallow. When she finally looked over at him, her eyes were troubled, wistful. But she nodded.

Chapter Thirteen

Swishing water over the blade, Jethro tapped it on the corner of the sink basin to dislodge any shaving cream before raising it. He was always very careful shaving around the scar. The last thing he wanted was to nick it and make it even more pronounced. He'd prefer not to shave the area at all, and to grow a mustache. But although Amish men grew beards when they married, mustaches were forbidden, because along with the fact that they were associated with the military that'd persecuted early Amish centuries ago, they were considered *hochmut*.

He supposed that might be true as it was surely pride that tempted him to grow one to cover the scar. Opening his mouth to stretch the skin above his lip taut, he began to shave the area. He'd been told his first surgery, the one to join the lip, was when he was six weeks old. There'd been…what? Six or seven others since then?

Lowering the razor, Jethro scowled into the mirror. His nose was still asymmetrical. People didn't seem as aware of it as he was. Or were mature enough not to mention it. Still, he was glad that, save the one in the bathroom, there weren't any mirrors in the house.

Most of the surgeries had been when he was younger. He didn't remember them. Except once when he'd been in the hospital and old enough to notice there were those with more obvious scars than his. Since then he'd learned there are some scars that were more on their soul than their physical being. Something perhaps less easily healed than split skin.

Well, his scars or his stammer couldn't define him if he didn't let them. Was he going to continue to? Susannah didn't seem to mind and that's what mattered. He loved her. The shoulders in the mirror rose and fell in a deep breath at the acknowledgment. Being with her these past few weeks had taken a respect and affection and cemented it into so much more. She made him happy. It was a novel feeling. He was determined to make her feel the same way.

So he'd better not blow this date. He set the

razor down with a shaking hand. Other than taking a female out to dinner, one who'd been forewarned by his parents to accept, his dating experience was limited.

Already knowing he was going to be baptized and join the church, Jethro's *rumspringa* had been short. Since Jethro hadn't thought he'd marry, there'd been no point in a long running-around period. He'd had no desire to go to singings and frolics, and even less to face rejection should he have asked to take a girl home afterward.

The girls had the pick of many other men in the community before they'd consider him. Jethro ran a thumb over the scar above his lip. His parents had never mentioned anyone in their family history with it, but he'd always wondered if his cleft was genetic and if there were risks in passing it on. Still, he'd been stunned and overjoyed when Louisa had reluctantly mentioned she was pregnant. When he'd lost them, he'd been lost for a bit, too. The babe had been his chance to be a father, even though the notion had petrified him.

Jerking the plug from the sink, Jethro drained his shaving water and ran a bit more to splash over his face. If only painful memories could be washed away like clumps of shaving cream. Casting a final look in the mirror, he grimaced as he touched the ends of his hair. His bowl cut was curling up at the ends. It needed to be cut again. Not that it mattered, but he wanted to look nice. At least as nice as possible.

Good thing he hadn't thought ahead about asking her for a date. If he had, he'd have been too nervous to get the words out. Although he could tell Susannah had been reluctant to do so, to his elation, she'd said yes. Well, nodded it, anyway. Jethro wanted to keep her in the habit of saying yes. There was a bigger question down the road, if he could work up the nerve to ask it, that he was hoping she'd say yes to as well. One that would make this courtship no longer fake.

The fact that some folks hadn't seemed to notice that they were courting, puzzled him. If Jethro had anything to do with it, this was the day they would definitely put that ignorance to rest.

Jethro's nervousness surged anew when Susannah settled next to him on the buggy seat. She looked so neat and vibrant in her white cap and apron over the dark green dress visible under her light jacket.

"Are you looking for anything in particular today?" As if noting the way his eyes feasted on her, a hint of pink flushed Susannah's complexion.

"B-besides m-making sure I'm seen with you? *Ja*. Looking for a new b-buggy for m-my *d-daed*."

"Surely he's not expecting you to replace it." Susannah eyed him with concern. "The wreck wasn't your fault."

"*Nee*. He's b-buying it. I'm just looking them over t-to advise the b-best choices for him t-to b-bid on."

Susannah nodded. "He trusts your judgment."

Jethro's smile froze for a moment before disappearing completely as he replayed the words the bishop had spoken to him regarding the woman currently seated on his left side. *It isn't Gott's will that you marry Susannah.* His grip tightened on the leather in his hands.

"On this matter, anyway." Jethro rolled his shoulders. The bishop would be there today. He would see them. That was *partly* the intent of this outing. To show his father that he would make his own decisions. Jethro inhaled sharply. He wasn't going to let his father bother him. An elemental joy hummed within him at spending the day with Susannah.

"I'm going to look at the ponies." Amos poked his head over the seat back into the space between Jethro and Susannah. The empty space Jethro longed to bridge by linking his hand with hers.

"Don't go thinking we're going to replace Ginger." Susannah turned to remind her son.

"Ah, Ginger is okay. Just because you want to look at something new doesn't mean you're not happy with what you have." The boy rested his arms across the leather. "I just like to look at ponies."

Jethro enjoyed the chatter between mother and son. "Why does someone who doesn't like to b-bake name her horses after spices?"

"Says the man who drives a horse named Cocoa," Susannah teased. "For me, it was the one place I knew what to do with them."

"That's right. You use m-more ingredients on the farm than in the kitchen."

With a smile, Susannah glanced over her shoulder at the other passenger in the back seat. "Anything in particular you'll be looking at, Rebecca?"

Amos snorted with the disgust of a younger brother. "She's just coming so she can look at the *youngies*."

"I am not!" The retort, followed by an affronted sniff, was instant. "I want to check out the crafts, particularly the quilts."

Jethro suppressed a smile at Rebecca's protest. From casual observations of her at social gatherings and the restaurant where she worked, he knew she wasn't averse to looking at men her age. He swiveled his head to see, like her mother previously, the young woman's pretty cheeks were flushed. The sight brought back another admonishment from his father—that he should look toward the daughter instead of the mother for a spouse. Jethro had no doubt that Rebecca would make someone a fine wife someday, but it wasn't going to be him.

"And maybe stop at the bake sale to see what they have."

Jethro turned back in time to see Susannah's lips twitch at her daughter's subtle nudge.

"*Ja, Mamm.* Can we get a cake or cookies so we can have something *gut* at home for once?"

The twitch morphed into a wry grimace at the reminder of her nonexistent baking skills. Susannah sighed. "You may choose one item each."

Jethro felt like sighing as well. In contentment. He was part of a family. A happy, teasing family. At least for the day. And if he could somehow convince the woman sitting next to him he was worthy, he would be a permanent member. Jethro's eyes widened. If things went as he hoped and Susannah married him, he'd become father to the two seated behind him. A father. Jethro shifted the lines to one hand to press a palm to his mouth. When Louisa and his *boppeli* had died, the unexpected hope of being a father that'd grown with his wife's pregnancy had died with them. Even though they weren't of his body, he would be proud to be a father to these fine young people.

"Are you all right, Jethro?"

He looked over at Susannah's quiet question. Because it was worth taking the risk, he surreptitiously reached out to grasp her slender hand that rested between them on the seat. She smiled at him quizzically. But Jethro's heart thrilled when she held it for several heartbeats before pulling free.

Faint heat rose up Susannah's neck when Jethro helped her down from the buggy. And she let him. It wasn't as if she hadn't climbed down from a buggy by herself a hundred—*nee,* a thousand times before. The flush rose higher when she saw all the interested gazes that turned their way.

This is why we came together today, after all. Although she shouldn't have agreed. She should've followed her better nature and let him go. Let him pursue a more suitable relationship. But when she was with Jethro, when he smiled in that shy, hopeful way…surely a little more time with him wouldn't hurt? She'd told him other women would welcome his attention, certainly that was enough? As he now knew he had other options, if he wanted to pursue them, he'd break it off with her, wouldn't he? But instead, he'd asked her to join him today, further cementing their charade. Susannah tried, and failed, to suppress the joy that thrummed through her at the knowledge.

Once out of the buggy, Amos and Rebecca hastily went their separate ways. Glancing at her, Jethro gestured to the stream of people walking toward the tents and assortments of good in the short distance. "B-business first?"

Nodding, Susannah fell into step beside him. When they located the used buggies for sale, Jethro went over each one, carefully examining them while Susannah visited with nearby friends whose husbands did the same. When Jethro returned to her side and indicated he was ready to go whenever she was, a few eyes widened. But it was the smiles that widened when the glances shifted between the two of them that thrilled Susannah.

A smile took up permanent residence on her face as they sauntered, arms or elbows occasionally brushing—each "accidental" bump sending happy jolts through Susannah. By tacit agreement, when Jethro spotted his father, she hung back, drifting over to the booth of baked goods while he went with the bishop to point out the buggies he'd recommend. Before she turned to stare at the breads, cookies and doughnuts, she saw the bishop narrow his eyes when he spied her nearby. But he didn't say anything. At least, not directly. But what might he say to Jethro? The thrill abated as she tucked a wayward strand of hair behind her ear.

"I set aside what Amos picked out. He stopped by earlier, saying you were letting him choose one."

Susannah looked up to see Ruth Schrock's grinning face. She arched an eyebrow. "I noticed no one asked me to contribute to the sale."

Ruth mirrored her expression. "I noticed you found other things to keep you busy." She glanced in the direction of where Jethro was walking with his father.

Susannah's gaze followed the pair as well. When they disappeared in the crowd, she turned back to Ruth. "Am I being foolish?"

The auburn-haired woman put her hands on her hips. "Susannah Mast, you are the least foolish person I know, and that includes myself."

"Denki." Susannah exhaled through pursed lips. "It's just that he's…"

"That he's a *gut* man and you, not being foolish, recognize that?"

"Ach, he could do so much better than me."

Ruth handed her a bag of cookies that bore a tag with the name Amos Mast. "Maybe as a baker. But not as a wife and partner." When Susannah reached for some money, Ruth shook her head. "It's on me. Although I know we're not supposed to have one, you need something to feed your ego. I know you'll make him very happy, and I can see that he's already doing that for you."

It was true. Relieved more than she could admit by Ruth's words, Susannah smiled gratefully. Before she could leave the table, another woman stepped up beside her. It was Linda Esh, who'd inquired about Susannah's matchmaking services for her daughter at the cleaning frolic. And specifically mentioned the bishop's son.

"I see that Jethro Weaver is here today. He's looking particularly fine. Have you had a chance to talk with him yet?"

Susannah opened her mouth but nothing came forth. Glancing over, she caught Ruth's droll gaze. Closing her mouth, Susannah cleared her throat. *"Ja.* I've been talking with him ever since he picked me up to go to the auction with him today."

The woman narrowed her eyes. With a pointed look at the bakery items on the table and the bag in Susannah's hand, she muttered, "At least my daughter could feed him," then stomped away. Susannah turned away as well, but not before an outrageous wink from Ruth prompted her to smile.

The smile expanded when she saw Jethro coming toward her. Susannah had to agree with Linda. Jethro was looking particularly fine. His blue eyes were so kind, so steady. Lit with frequently unspoken humor if you shared a glance at the right time. Like the one they were sharing now. Susannah curled her fingers more tightly around the bag of cookies to ensure she didn't reach for his hand.

"Finished?"

"With that. B-but not with the t-time I want t-to spend with you." With a brief touch of his hand on her arm, they melted back into the crowd.

It took more than a few miles on the trip home for Amos to finish talking about his adventures that day. And probably only then because his mouth was full of the cookies. Susannah let him eat his fill as Rebecca shared her day. When she'd ended her stories and leaned back, Susannah snuck a glance at Jethro. And found him looking back at her.

It'd been a wonderful day. The best day. They'd giggled like children together. They'd talked with good friends as if they were a couple. They'd avoided his parents and anyone else who'd looked at them askance. There'd been very few who had. When Jethro laid his hand palm up on the seat between them, Susannah didn't hesitate to entwine hers with it. And treasure his grasp the rest of the way home.

She'd started the day worried that encouraging this mock courtship was the wrong thing to do. Now she was wondering how to make it real. Because to her, it was. Her breath hitched as Jethro gently ran his thumb over the back of her hand. The amazing thing was that he seemed to want that, too. Susannah slowly exhaled. This wasn't part of their plan. But plans could be changed, couldn't they?

Chapter Fourteen

❧

Jethro did another quick count of the bags on the wagon, ensuring the number matched what he'd calculated as he'd loaded them. Upon confirmation, he reentered the back door of the feed store to pay. His steps paused when he saw the older man and woman at the counter. He smiled faintly. Mrs. Danvers, who'd worked with him when he'd gone to the *Englisch* grammar school, hadn't changed much over the years. Although pleased to see her—he'd always greatly respected his speech teacher—Jethro didn't want to visit. But even though he stayed in the back of the store stacked high with bags of different kinds of animal feed, the alert woman caught sight of him. With a brief word to her companion, she headed his way.

Sliding his hands down the sides of his pants, Jethro tried to dry his suddenly sweaty palms. Would she expect him to be able to talk like he had as a student when they were meeting regularly? She had been so helpful. It shamed him that his speech had regressed since then. Particularly when he wanted to make a good impression. Which made him nervous, because he wanted to do so. Which affected his speech. It was a frustrating cycle. Shifting his feet, Jethro glanced longingly at his wagon. The store's proprietor could put this load on his bill. The man knew what he'd intended to pick up and that he was good for it. But it was too late…

"Jethro! How nice to see you."

Dry-mouthed, Jethro considered a greeting. *D* was one of the letters he'd always had issues with, along with *m*, *p*, *b* and *t*. Why couldn't her name have been Mrs. Stuart?

Perspiration trickled down the center of his back. "Hello," he finally inserted into the awkward silence.

If Mrs. Danvers noted his evasion, she didn't let on. She shared the kind smile he'd always remembered. "I was just talking about you the other day."

Immediately tensing, Jethro eyed her warily.

"I ran into Susannah Mast. I understand she's a good friend of yours."

The stiffness in his shoulders eased and Jethro gave an acknowledging nod. If anyone was to discuss him, he would rather it be Susannah. He knew he could trust her with his self-consciousness regarding his speech. After all, he feared he was already well on his way to trusting her with his heart. "*Ja.* She is."

"She indicated it would be good if you and I worked together on your speech again."

Jethro went rigid. His heart pounded in denial. He'd never known Mrs. Danvers to lie. Or to exaggerate the truth. Why would Susannah tell his old teacher the exact opposite of his expressed wishes the only time they'd discussed it? Was she ashamed of him now that folks truly thought they were a couple? Had she grown tired of listening to his stammer as they spent more time together? Crossing his arms tightly over his chest, Jethro stepped back.

"*Nee.* No," he repeated, just in case the *Englisch* woman didn't understand his original dialect. "I d-don't want any m-more lessons." His face heated as he stumbled over the words. Retreating farther, his escape ended when he bumped against a hip-high stack of cattle feed.

Mrs. Danvers' smile faded. Her brow creased with concern, but she nodded mildly as if she knew when to withdraw as well. "It was just a thought. If you're ever interested, I'd be happy to work with you. Since retirement, my husband and I are looking for anything to keep us active and out of each other's hair. Something you're probably not familiar with as I'm sure you're always busy." Jethro wanted to wince under her compassionate gaze. "And probably are now, so I'll let you go. It was very nice to see you again, Jethro." With a graceful smile, she returned to where the older man waited for her at the store's front door.

Jethro quickly paid his bill and left the store. On the way home, his stomach felt as if the load of feed in the wagon behind him sat upon it. And upon his heart. He'd trusted Susannah. She'd been the only woman he'd ever trusted and loved. Well, that would teach him. His shoulders sagged despondently until it seemed they should be resting on his thighs instead of his elbows.

As he couldn't trust his own choices, he might as well do what his folks wanted him to do. At least then he wouldn't have to bear their disapproving glares, comments or reproachful silences. His mouth twisted. They'd give him some time to dwell on his own poor choice before the I-told-you-so lecture, one followed shortly by instructions on when and whom to court.

Jethro stared between the ears of his draft

horses to the road ahead, seeing his future as gray and unchanging as the pavement under their plodding hooves. Under his parents' pressure, he knew he'd eventually marry again. The thought made his stomach churn further. The woman would be a wise choice, according to his parents. But for sure and certain, not someone he loved.

The lines drooped in his hands. Good thing he didn't have to worry about the Belgians going anywhere. Jethro shook his head morosely. He could live without love. He'd done it before. It was just…he'd been happy. With Susannah in his life, the sun seemed brighter, his burdens lighter. He'd never felt that way before.

Maybe there'd been some mistake? Some misunderstanding? He straightened in the seat at the possibility. Surely it would be reasonable to see her and determine the truth? Better than letting hurt and fear fester on some simple misinterpretation. Reaching the corner for her road, Jethro turned the Belgians. By the time he swung them up her lane, the weight of both the big draft animals seemed to be resting on his chest as well as the feed. When he saw Susannah working in the garden with her own team, he set the wagon's brake and stiffly climbed down.

She waved when she saw him. A greeting he didn't return. When she reached the end of the row, Jethro closed the distance.

"*Guder daag.* I didn't expect to see you today. Although I'm glad I am. What brings you by?" Her smile accompanied the words as she bent to clear dried vines from the machinery.

"I saw M-Mrs. D-Danvers in t-town t-to-day." Jethro gritted out the words.

"*Ja*? I ran into her the other day at the Dew Drop."

"So she said."

Apparently alerted by his tone, Susannah stopped what she was doing. Dusting off her hands, she straightened to give Jethro her full attention.

"D-did you t-tell her that she should work with m-me on m-my speech?"

Her eyes shifted. The brown eyes he'd loved and trusted shifted as they acknowledged what he'd said. Jethro's hope faded as his heart sank.

"*Ja.* I told her that it would be *gut*. That it might…help you."

At least she didn't lie. But each word was a blow to Jethro. Each word reinforced the knowledge that she didn't find him worthy as he was.

"Everyone seems t-to have an opinion on

what is *gut* for m-me. Like I'm incapable of d-deciding for m-myself." His voice was hoarse. Jethro swallowed against the ache in his throat. "I thought you were *gut* for m-me. B-but apparently I'm not *gut* for you. Or m-maybe just not *gut* enough."

Every remembered mockery of his speech stabbed at him. He'd thought she'd been different. That she hadn't minded his speech. His mistake, in letting himself care for someone.

"Jethro, it's not that at all." To her credit, Susannah looked stricken. Considering him silently, she sighed heavily.

And what did the sigh mean? That he was trying her patience, as if he were a child or imbecile? The notion struck Jethro almost as painfully as knowing his speech bothered her.

"You're trying to pick a quarrel." A corner of Susannah's lip tipped up in a smile, although it was a trembling one. "Two cannot quarrel when one will not."

Jethro didn't want to hear the old Amish platitude. "I'm not quarrelling. I'm t-trying t-to understand why the only woman I t-t-t…" Closing his eyes, he paused to take a deep breath; to continue as he was would only reinforce her obvious low opinion of him. "T-trusted…would b-be ashamed of me." Heat rose up his neck and flushed his cheeks.

"Would d-do exactly what I p-p-particularly d-determined not t-t-to." She was ashamed of him. The knowledge was agony.

"So if I can't even t-trust you, I m-might as well court some of those other women I've b-been t-told that I should b-be seeing. B-but spare m-me your newfound role, b-because I d-don't need you t-to b-be m-my m-matchmaker. I wanted you as m-my wi—" He struggled to swallow. "The last thing I want is t-to have you b-be m-my m-matchmaker."

Blinking rapidly as if there was something in her eyes, Susannah's compressed her lips into a thin, quavering line. "That would probably be for the best," she murmured huskily.

Nodding curtly, Jethro spun on his heel and strode to where he'd left the Belgians. Where he hoped he'd left them, because his vision was initially so blurred that he couldn't see clearly. Thankfully, his direction was good. Swiftly taking his seat, Jethro guided the draft team out of the farmyard.

Although he longed to look back, he didn't. He couldn't. The sooner he moved on from his mistake, the better. Or so his mind said. His heart said something different entirely. Fortunately, his mind was well accustomed to taking charge.

Which is why, as soon as he reached home

and unloaded the feed, Jethro reloaded the wagon with the plow Ben Raber had asked to borrow and drove it over to the neighboring farmstead that Ben was renting. Jethro didn't want to be alone with his fractured emotions. For once, he wanted company.

You'd always wanted Susannah's company. Jethro hushed his wounded heart.

As he entered the lane, Jethro saw that Ben's brother, Aaron, was there. It was an effective distraction. For the first time since the feed store, a faint smile touched his lips. He was glad the two brothers had reconciled.

Aaron had left their Amish community early last year. When Ben had abruptly married Rachel—long understood as Aaron's girlfriend—the community had been surprised. Probably none more so than Aaron when he'd returned to find his brother not only married to Rachel, but parenting twins with her. Fortunately, the brothers seemed to be getting along fine now. Although Ben was much more settled than the restless Aaron. *Maybe marriage did that. Settled you.* Although, Jethro hadn't really felt settled and content when married to Louisa. His throat clogged immediately. *I would be if I married Susannah.*

But that wasn't happening. He needed to look elsewhere. So when Jethro saw a woman he knew was single hanging up the wash in the Rabers' yard, he asked her out.

The moment they'd sat down at the Dew Drop, Jethro was already wishing he hadn't come. Already wishing that he was either at home or at Susannah's. But that wasn't an option any more.

"Is something wrong?"

He looked up to find his date's curious gaze on him. "*Nee.*" Jethro rubbed a hand over his face. There was nothing wrong other than his heart was broken. Surely it would recover. Although he couldn't imagine when.

Inviting Miriam Schrock to dinner had been a mistake. He hadn't had an appetite ever since his and Susannah's discussion. *Discussion* seemed too pleasant a word for something so painful. Or so foolish. Because what if she hadn't really meant it the way he'd taken it? What if it hadn't really been that at all, like she'd said? *Ja,* this whole thing had been a mistake. The only thing he wanted to eat right now were the words he'd spoken to her in hurt and anger. He'd even happily eat some of Susannah's awful cookies, as long as she was there beside him.

Glasses of water appeared on the table between him and Miriam. When Jethro glanced up, he almost sank through the booth at the sight of Rebecca's impassive face. The usually vivacious girl was totally devoid of expression. He'd forgotten Susannah's daughter waitressed here. At the curious look of the woman across from him, he opened his mouth. It was a few moments before any sound came out. *"D-d-denki."* Jethro dropped his head as embarrassing heat rushed up his neck and into his cheeks. He clenched his fingers around the menu.

"Are you ready to order? Or do you want a few minutes?" Rebecca's tone was as stiff as her face.

Jethro's stomach knotted. What he wanted was to leave. He was betraying Susannah by being there. He was betraying himself. He'd been *hochmut*. It was pride that'd gotten him into this. Pride that'd wrecked the best thing that had ever happened to him.

"Maybe a few minutes would be *gut*." Rebecca nodded and left at Miriam's quiet words. Jethro shot an appreciative glance across the table. Miriam didn't deserve this. He shouldn't have involved her in this…this—whatever this was.

Earlier this afternoon, so tightly twisted up inside he was surprised he could stay upright on the wagon's seat, Jethro had walked straight over to where Miriam Schrock was hanging up the laundry. He didn't know who was more surprised when he stopped in front of her. Her, him or the watching Raber brothers.

He hadn't wanted to ask out any of the women who might've been asking after him. He didn't want it thought by Susannah or anyone that she was acting as his matchmaker. But before he lost his nerve, he'd wanted to ask someone, as he'd proclaimed to Susannah that he would. And Jethro knew Miriam wouldn't have been on the list.

Miriam had recently arrived in the area to be a hired girl for Rachel and her twins. Hopefully, she was similar in personality to her brothers. Jethro was friends with Malachi, Samuel and their younger brother, Gideon. When he'd haltingly asked her to dinner, her eyes had widened. After stating that she'd need to ask Rachel first, Miriam went to do so while he and the Raber brothers unloaded the plow. When she'd returned, after a hooded gaze at Aaron, she confirmed that Jethro had a dinner date.

Now guilt swamped him at involving Miriam in his troubles. Would his spontaneous action affect his relationship with the Schrocks? Wouldn't that just be great? In one fell swoop, he would wreck his friendship with Susannah and sabotage the one with the Schrocks.

"Why did you ask me out?"

Jethro cringed. For sure and certain, Miriam was more straightforward than her brothers.

"Did you and Susannah have a fight? I won't be used to make someone jealous."

That was far from his intent. Jethro had wanted to assure himself that other women thought enough of him to date him. Was that trying to make Susannah jealous? The concept was alien to him. The only association he'd ever had with jealousy had been his feeling toward his little brother, Atlee. Atlee, who'd been perfect and cherished by their parents. No matter what Jethro had done, he hadn't garnered similar reactions. After a while, he'd quit trying to please them, determining to simply do things that he'd thought were right.

But wasn't he doing just as his folks had wished? Ending his relationship with Susannah and courting someone they'd consider more appropriate?

Jethro grew cold at the realization. He wanted to beat his head on the table. Instead, he shook it miserably.

"*Nee*," he muttered belatedly.

Miriam gave him a sympathetic smile. "Do you really feel like having dinner?"

Jethro smiled glumly. When the woman he'd asked out to a meal recognized he didn't want to be there, it proved that he was a disaster at courting. His shoulders dropped in defeat. "Not really. I apologize, M-Miriam. This hasn't b-been m-much of a d-date."

She slid out of the booth. "That's all right. You can make it up to me by stopping at the Dairy Mart to pick up some food on the way out of town."

"I'll b-be glad t-to d-do that." Tossing enough bills on the table to cover his embarrassment in entering the restaurant in the first place, he followed Miriam out the door.

Her matter-of-fact conversation interspersed with periods of companionable silence helped steady Jethro on the way home. Miriam was a wonderful girl, which Jethro was certain the local single men would soon discover. But she wasn't for him. There was only one woman for him.

And he'd just destroyed any chance for a relationship with her.

Chapter Fifteen

Susannah shifted on the hard bench. Ordination Sunday was always particularly long. Normally, she loved church. But today she'd rather be home, still quietly grieving over her and Jethro's parting the other day. How had it all gone so wrong?

She straightened when a hush descended in the barn. Bishop Weaver and Minister John Stoltzfus were returning after being cloistered following the church members' voting to fill the ministerial vacancy. Watching them, Susannah furrowed her brow. Although their expressions matched the solemnity of the occasion, the bishop looked unsettled. Almost as unsettled as herself. Preventing her gaze from finding Jethro on the men's benches where they sat opposite the women in the barn had been more difficult that she could've imagined.

It was even worse when it invariably settled on him like a bee returning to its hive. More devastating was to find him looking back, his dear face so grave, his blue eyes shadowed. She'd spent more time with downcast eyes this service than she had the whole year to date. As the day continued, lead had settled in her stomach. *Gut* thing she'd have another two weeks before church was held again. Maybe by then it wouldn't hurt so bad to see him. Susannah bit her cheek. Or to hear in the meantime that he was now actively courting others. She didn't know who'd needed more comfort the other day when Rebecca had come home from the Dew Drop after having seen Jethro there with another woman—her or her daughter. If she had wondered whether her children supported their relationship, she now knew they had. Fully. She wished she'd told them the truth about the fake courtship. But then, toward the end, she'd denied the truth herself.

She forced her attention to where Bishop Weaver was laying five *Ausbunds*—denoting five candidates—side by side on the table set up between the men's and women's benches. Even though she didn't have a husband who might have to select one of the hymnals today, Susannah's heart started pounding. Amish believed a minister was chosen by *Gott*. That He would lead the appropriate candidate to select the hymnal containing a bible verse, a selection confirming that man into the life of minister, perhaps later, even bishop, whether the man sought the role or not.

Bishop Weaver visibly swallowed. "The candidates for minister receiving three or more votes are…" The barn was preternaturally quiet. It was as if those present had ceased breathing for a moment. Even the pigeons in the loft, cooing earlier to the amusement of some during the church service, were silent. Susannah understood. The job was a blessing. It was also a burden. The job was unpaid, untrained and for a lifetime. And ministers were expected to speak without notes for twenty minutes to an hour on Sundays, not knowing which sermon he'd be preaching until just prior to the service.

Everyone waited to hear the names, afraid that theirs, or their spouse's, would be mentioned. A glance down her row revealed more than one of her married bench mates had reached out to grasp the hand of a nearby friend.

Bishop Weaver cleared his throat. When a *boppeli* in one of the young mother's arms emitted a small cry, there was a ripple through the congregation as everyone tensed.

"Isaiah Zook." Even in the challenging acoustics of the barn, the bishop's hoarse voice was easily heard in the hush. Susannah followed the turn of heads on the other side to find the dairyman. He was staring straight ahead, his expression set.

"Malachi Schrock." A sharp inhalation from the row behind her identified the location of where the furniture business owner's wife sat with their young daughter.

"Elmer Raber." Susannah winced fractionally when she heard Ben's *daed's* name. Elmer was a quiet, reserved man. If chosen, the role would weigh heavily on him.

"Henry Troyer." A widower of a few years, Henry was a pleasant man and successful farmer. Although his sons were doing fine in the community, his older daughters had given him some trials of late. One lived separately from her husband, although on the same property. Another had moved out of state after her heavy pursuit of a potential spouse had driven all the men away.

Without Jethro and her fake courtship, Henry might've been one who'd eventually come calling. Susannah swallowed. When word was broadcast that their relationship was over, he might come calling still. If he did, she'd find some way to dissuade him. After what she'd almost had with Jethro, *nee*, she didn't want to court anyone.

"And Jethro Weaver."

Susannah's breath froze in her lungs. Her ears began ringing. Aware of exactly where he was sitting, her gaze shot to Jethro. His face was so white, the faint scar showed in contrast. His eyes locked with hers. She wanted to weep at the despair in them. To race between the benches separating the men and women and throw her arms around him.

While the rest of the congregation was motionless, there was subtle movement in the third row behind Jethro. Her tense gaze shifted in time to see smirks on the faces of three young men, ones recently baptized. Susannah's suspended breath exhaled in a rush. *Oh, you young fools. You don't know what you've done.* She knew what this role would do to Jethro. Although a godly man, it was the last position he wanted. Splinters of the worn plank pricked into the palms of her white-knuckled grip of the bench. Susannah's gaze darted back to Jethro as he slowly rose to take his place with the other candidates at the center of the barn.

One by one, the men selected their hymnals in the order they'd been called, leaving Jethro with no choice at all. Even so, he hesitated, his shoulders rigid under his *mutza* suit as he picked up the last hymnal from the table. Trudging back to his seat, he sat cautiously, as if he was afraid the bench, as well as his world, had shifted from beneath him.

Susannah understood, particularly having been a minister's wife. And that had been to a man who'd become more than comfortable with the role. Vernon had grown to relish preaching on Sunday. She'd wondered at the time if he'd taken some inappropriate pride in appearing more spiritual than others.

Jethro would never enjoy preaching, even without the stutter. He'd also be totally ill at ease in counseling those out of line with the *Ordnung's* rules.

Heart pounding so frantically she could feel it pulse at the tips of her fingers, Susannah watched as the bishop nodded for the candidates to open their hymnals. One by one, in the order they'd selected them, they did so. The rustle of pages could be heard as Isaiah Zook opened his book. When no slip of scripture was found, his shoulders sagged in relief. A soft exhalation came from along Susannah's bench, where Isaiah's wife sat.

While the dairy farmer was obviously relieved, the tension grew for the remaining four men on the bench. All attention now focused on Malachi Schrock. The young man's face was expressionless, but a bead of perspiration tracked down the side of his brow. Opening his hymnal's cover, he slowly flipped through the pages. When no piece of paper was found, the furniture maker's eyes closed at his reprieve. This time, there was no mistaking the muffled squeak from the row behind Susannah as Ruth Schrock shared her husband's relief.

Elmer Raber's hands shook as he spread wide the book in his lap. As he paged through it to find no note, he started breathing so rapidly, Susannah would've been concerned for the older man if she wasn't so afraid for the man she loved.

Why it would take a moment like this to make her realize it, Susannah didn't wonder. All she knew was that she ached to wrap her arms around him. Ached to comfort and support his tense figure. Breathing so shallowly she was lightheaded herself, she did what she could. She held his gaze. She wanted to shout the words to give him strength but knew that was the last thing she could do. She wanted to take his burdens away, share this one for the lifetime it would be, if that's what he needed.

It was down to just two. Henry Troyer's book wobbled on his knees as he opened it. When he slowly fanned the pages, there was a communal gasp as a slip of paper fluttered to the barn floor. Henry grimaced, his previously pale face turning red. His eyes filled with tears.

Susannah's breath finally normalized as she watched Jethro reach over and grip the man's shoulder in a consoling clasp. As Henry struggled to compose himself, Jethro withdrew his hand and, with a deep breath, opened his own hymnal. When no notes revealed themselves, he closed it with a soft thud. His head tipped back and his throat bobbed in a heavy swallow.

A hand settled on Jethro's shoulder. Bishop Weaver stood behind his son, his head bowed. The material of Jethro's suit crinkled under the bishop's tightened fingers. Jethro reached up to pat his father's hand with his own. A huge sigh lifted Ezekiel Weaver's gaunt shoulders as he nodded before removing his hand. Susannah didn't know if a word had been spoken between the two men, but apparently the bishop was also relieved that Jethro hadn't been selected. Because he knew his son and didn't think he could do the job? Or because he knew the job and knew what taking on the role would do to his son? For Jethro's sake, she hoped the latter.

When Jethro lifted his head a moment later, he looked straight into Susannah's eyes. As their gazes locked, the obvious relief in his eyes shifted to a question. A question that brought Susannah's breathlessness back. But for a different reason. Because it wasn't for the role he'd just missed. It was for the role he wanted. Did she want it, too? Could she? Should she? Breaking eye contact, she stood from the bench when the service was over. Needing something to do with her hands, she brushed off the back of her skirt while she looked anywhere but at Jethro. Using the hasty excuse of needing to milk her goats after the lengthy service, she left for home, giving Amos a distracted permission to linger with a school friend.

Jethro drew the gelding to a halt in front of Susannah's front gate. His palms were sweating. Was he making a mistake? He was almost as nervous as he'd been earlier during the ordination. What if he'd misread her expression? What if the poignant gaze they'd shared when he'd been frightened beyond himself had been a delusion of his pounding heart and heightened senses? He'd searched for her but, like many others with livestock to care for, she'd left soon after the ordination service. Or was that why she'd left so soon? Had it been intentional, so she wouldn't have to see him? Jethro exhaled through pursed lips. Surely the bees in Susannah's hives weren't buzzing as much as the thoughts in his head.

He climbed down from the buggy and secured the gelding to the rail. Rubbing the back of his neck, he turned his attention to the front door. Should he look for her in the house, or would she still be in the barn doing chores? What should he say when he found her?

Guder owed, Susannah. I'm thinking you've forgotten or forgiven me for our recent discussion, because today you looked at me like you might...care for me so I hurried through chores so I could drop by to see if it was so. That didn't seem an appropriate start. Besides, with his stutter amplified by his tension, he would probably struggle through the lengthy sentence.

The front door swung open.

He'd have to think of something soon because wiping her hands on her apron as she stepped onto the porch was Susannah. Without hesitation, she headed down the walk toward him. Jethro stood transfixed as she came through the gate. He was still frozen when she walked up to him. He only began to melt when she wrapped her arms around him. Instinctively, reverently, Jethro returned her embrace. Eyes drifting closed, he rested his cheek against her prayer *kapp*. *I would strug-gle through giving a hundred hour-long sermons just to have this moment.*

"Oh, Jethro, I was so anxious for you. And the other day, when I spoke to Mrs. Danvers, I certainly didn't mean…"

"I know," he murmured into her hair. "I'm sorry I d-didn't t-trust you."

Jethro opened his eyes to see her upturned face. They met her soft gaze before dropping to her lips. Lips that he longed to kiss. Automatically dipping his head, he hesitated before drawing back. Who was he fooling? She wouldn't want his kisses. Louisa hadn't. And she'd been his wife. Keeping Susannah enfolded in his arms, he focused his attention on the porch behind her as he worried his top lip. He felt the bite of his teeth along its length, except for the section that had no feeling.

Jethro winced. "I'm not *gut* at this."

Susannah's eyes reflected her puzzlement. "At what?" She tightened her embrace. "You've proven yourself to be *gut* at anything. You'd even have been a *gut* minister, had you been chosen."

"I can't kiss."

She blinked in confusion before a slow grin spread over her face. "Is that a rule for bishops' sons?"

Although he thrilled at her teasing, his fear of her rejection was too great to respond to the joke. "*Nee*, my kisses aren't *gut*."

Susannah's smile abruptly faded as her brow creased over brown eyes turned fierce. "Who told you that?"

The admission was painful. "Louisa d-didn't like to kiss m-me."

Susannah cocked her head as she solemnly studied him. "That sounds like her problem."

"*Nee*. It is m-mine. Where m-my lip is joined, I d-don't have any feeling. I d-don't kiss well."

"*Ach*, let me be the judge of that." At his doubtful expression, her grin returned. "Maybe we should try and see. Perhaps, instead of your lips, it was the pairing of the two of you."

Jethro couldn't help but smile at her logic. Was it possible? He and Louisa had definitely not been a love match. But dare he try? Louisa rejecting him was one thing. He had married her out of duty, not out of affection. Whereas his feelings for Susannah… Jethro didn't think he could bear it if she rejected him as well. But could he bear to never kiss this woman?

His gaze knotted with Susannah's until, as both their eyes drifted shut, Jethro lowered his head and gently touched his lips to hers. Lifting his head a few moments later, years of fear that'd strangled the edges of his soul melted away when he opened his eyes to the look in Susannah's.

She tipped her head as her smile widened. "I think if you're unsure about it, you should keep practicing."

Again, he liked her logic. And so he did. When he raised his head a second time, Susannah sighed. Jethro knew it to be a contented one. One that he shared.

"You are definitely *gut* at this, Jethro Weaver."

Jethro felt good. Everything about this woman made him feel good. So good that he blurted out the words he'd never expected to say again. "Marry me."

Susannah's mouth rounded such that, had one of her honeybees been flying by, she'd have been in danger of inviting the creature in. Was her shock because she wanted to? Or because she didn't want to?

"You didn't stutter."

"My heart is m-making up for that. Marry me."

"Oh, Jethro. I don't know… This isn't what we planned."

"It m-may not b-be what we p-planned b-but it's what we want. Or, at least, what I want. T-today I was faced with t-taking on a role I'd have for the rest of m-my life. I've realized the role that I want for the rest of m-my life is t-to b-be your husband. Marry me, Susannah."

"It would be foolish. We'd be making a mistake."

"Okay then. M-make it with m-me. I've m-made others. This is one I'll happily live with."

Now it was Susannah who chewed on her lip. Then her fingertips. Followed by pressing both hands to her face until all that was revealed were her eyes. Eyes that wanted to say yes, Jethro could tell. But would she?

When finally, hesitantly, the word escaped through her fingers, Jethro thought his heart would burst with joy.

Chapter Sixteen

❧

Jethro ran the comb over the Belgian's sweaty hide. He felt good about what he and the team had accomplished today. This would finish the field work for him for the year, freeing him up even more to help others where needed. Primarily Susannah, although he knew from what he'd done earlier that her work should be almost completed as well. Too bad. It was a handy excuse to see her.

At the clatter of buggy wheels coming up the lane, he paused. His head lifted at the sound, closely followed by his pulse rate. Was it Susannah? He hadn't wanted to leave her yesterday. The memory of their shared embrace lingered on his lips. In his arms. In his heart. His face creased with a smile. Maybe she missed him as much as he missed her.

With an eager step, Jethro strode for the barn door. Swinging it open, he stepped out and—

What was his mother doing here? Once again, Jethro's pulse surged, but for an entirely different reason. It was accompanied by a tightening in his stomach. If she was going to try to talk him out of seeing Susannah, she'd wasted the trip over. He ducked back into the shadows of the barn but guilt swept over him at his cowardice. Leaning out the door, he waved so she'd know where he was before he went back to work. By the time the Belgian he was grooming swung his head toward the door, indicating the unwanted company had arrived, Jethro had made sure he was on the far side of the gigantic cream-colored horse.

He didn't speak, just continued running the brush and rubber comb over the horse's broad shoulder, smoothing out hair that'd become matted with sweat under the harness collar. In the silence unbroken except for the rhythmic sweeps of the tools on the horse's hide, he waited, shoulders hitched, for his *mamm* to say what she wanted, as surely she would. She always had. He waited. And waited. And waited.

Having brushed this side of the horse so thoroughly the animal would probably glow in the dark, Jethro sighed. Reluctantly, he worked his way around the gelding until he was on the same side as his mother. Shooting a wary glance over his shoulder, he saw her quietly sitting on a bale of straw, hands folded in her lap as she watched him. It was unsettling. Jethro's usually fluid motions were stiff in the continued quiet. The Belgian nudged him with his gigantic head at the odd behavior, almost knocking him over.

"Your *grossdaddi*, my father, died before you were born."

Jethro paused in midstroke at her flat statement. Whatever he'd been expecting her to say, it wasn't this.

"You never knew him. Or my younger *bruder*."

He turned fully to face her. He'd never heard that his *mamm* had a younger *bruder*. He'd heard said that his *grossmammi* had died in childbirth and that his *grossdaddi* had never remarried after her death. But when no word had ever been mentioned of siblings on his *mamm's* side, he assumed she'd died when his *mamm* was born.

"I was eight when my *bruder* was born. It wasn't spoken of then. Still isn't." Her thin face reddened a bit. "But I think my *mamm* lost several *boppeli* between me and him. And when Atlee was born, we lost her."

Jethro frowned. Furrowing his brow, he

crossed his arms over his chest. "Atlee?" It'd been his younger *bruder's* name. His perfect, pampered, younger *bruder*. His deceased younger *bruder* who'd left a widow whom Jethro had married to take care of. At his *mamm's* insistence.

His mother's face was stiff. "Your younger *bruder* was named for mine."

Jethro slumped against the Belgian. Fortunately, the horse stood firm as a living wall.

"I understand Susannah Mast was stung by some ground-nesting yellow jackets."

Tensing at Susannah's name, Jethro was ready to defend her should his *mamm* say anything derogatory. Where was his mother going with this? Why, after all this time…? His eyes widened at the sight of her white knuckles, visible in her clenched hands. In the silence, her shoulders lifted in a deep inhale.

"My father was a hard worker. He expected everyone else to be as well. He was a…tough taskmaster. I learned to do everything successfully. Even take care of my little *bruder*.

"One day when my *vader* was gone, my *bruder* went out to mow the hay. At seven, and small for his age, he was too little to do it by himself. He wouldn't have been able to, if I hadn't helped him harness the team. I shouldn't have. But he wanted to do it. He wanted to pull his own weight, he said. He wanted to do something helpful for *Vader*. Atlee knew, as I knew, that *Vader* was disappointed in him."

She looked down at her tightly entwined hands. "Whereas I did everything *Vader* asked, and even more so as I got older and wise enough to anticipate him, Atlee didn't. He dawdled. He daydreamed. He was sickly. It was surprising he survived infancy, as I was the one taking care of him, and I didn't know what I was doing, never having been around a new *boppeli* before. Fortunately, a neighbor came over frequently to check on him. And me. And we got by. The two of us got by better than Atlee and my father did. Not only did Atlee have to be told twice to do something, he had to be told through me. *Vader* didn't even want to talk with Atlee. You see… Atlee stuttered."

Jethro froze. He was barely able to breathe as he stood there listening. The Belgian behind him stomped his bucket-sized foot on the floor. Jethro felt the reverberation through his work boots, but the sound didn't register because all his hearing was focused on what his mother was saying from where she sat on the bale.

"So I helped him harness the team that day. We had Belgians as well." Her eyes remained downcast. "Big, strong horses. I watched him drive the team out to the field with the mower. Figured it would be *gut,* like Atlee thought, to have *Vader* come home and see the work finished. Maybe be able to tell *Vader* what he'd done himself. I went back to the house to work. I looked out the window from time to time to check on him."

His *mamm* seemed fascinated with a blade of straw that'd escaped from the bale. She ran the toe of her black shoe over it, rolling the blade back and forth until she pressed so hard one end of the blade lifted off the barn floor. When she spoke again, her voice was hoarse. "I never imagined they'd drive over a yellow jacket nest. The horses panicked with the stings. Atlee couldn't handle them. It all went wrong." Her face paled. The only evidence of where her lips were was a telltale quiver.

Jethro tilted his head forward to hear her last whispered words.

"I didn't protect him when I should've."

He needed to sit. Stumbling away from the horse's side, Jethro sagged against the stall wall. He continued to slide down the rough wood until he rested on the barn floor, his back braced against the boards.

"Shortly after your father and I married, he was chosen as minister. Thanks to my upbringing, even though I was a young bride, I knew I could handle the role. I was going to be an exceptional minister's wife." She hunched a shoulder. "I succeeded. When the previous bishop died in the following year, Ezekiel was chosen to replace him. It's an esteemed role, a weighty responsibility in the district. I was going to do everything to help make him a successful bishop and do all that was right as a bishop's wife."

She looked over to where Jethro, knees drawn up with his arms around them, had propped himself against the stall wall. "You were born shortly after he took the position. I was excited to be a mother. I was going to care for you like I hadn't been able to care for my *bruder*."

Her gaze shifted away. "It was…obvious from the moment you were born that you were going to need some help. We knew we'd have to take you to a hospital. Especially when we couldn't get you to eat. With the cleft…"

Jethro hissed in a breath when his *mamm's* face crumpled. He'd never seen her as anything other than stern and daunting. She quickly regained control. If he hadn't been watching, he wouldn't have seen it. "I couldn't nurse you. I wasn't able to feed you. Not even with a bottle. I'd successfully undertaken every other role, but I couldn't take care of my own child. We took you to a local hospital. They sent you to the large one in Madison. I couldn't stay with you. I sat at home, all ready for a baby. But had no baby for a week. They finally sent you home with special bottles that had special nipples that you could handle. Several weeks later, you had your first surgery to close the split in your lip.

"Things improved, as you could at least eat. But when you had cereal for the first time..." She shook her head. "You had no roof of your mouth. As you explored the strange texture with your tongue and tried to figure out what to do with it, it all came back out your nose. I'd always been able to do everything. But I couldn't effectively take care of my own child. Like I didn't with my little brother."

Plucking straw out of the bale on which she sat, she picked at the golden blades. "Like most Amish, we don't carry health insurance. As a community, we take care of each other. But it was everyone taking care of us. All the time. There were so many surgeries. None of them nearby. You had to stay at those places overnight. Every one cost thousands of dollars. As the district's church leader, we should've been helping others. But it wasn't that way. For years, it was always us the community was constantly holding fundraisers for. I was ashamed to have cost the district so much work and money."

Jethro's mouth was dry. He tightened his grip of his knees as if to hold himself together. It was such a different conversation than the one he'd expected when he'd seen her rig drive up the lane. His *mamm* had never spoken of this to him. He wasn't sure what to do with the unexpected history. It explained many things, but it didn't erase the loneliness of his childhood.

For a moment, his *mamm* held his gaze before dropping hers back into her lap. "When Atlee…" She swallowed. "When your *bruder,* Atlee, was born, I didn't feel like I didn't know what to do, like when my little *bruder* was a *boppeli,* or that I wasn't enough, like when you were. I could take care of him. I was going to protect him, like I hadn't my *bruder,* or you, when you were always taken from me to have the surgeries that brought you back swollen and bruised." She wore a sad smile. "And I did. Maybe too well. As you turned out better without my help, than he did with it."

Her mouth twisted ruefully. "Susannah Mast told me that. She said the man you'd become is more a credit to you than me. She also said I didn't deserve you."

The heels of Jethro's boots skidded along the barn floor as he abruptly straightened his legs. Susannah had said that? Far from being ashamed of him as he'd mistakenly thought, she'd been defending him to his mother? His lips curved in a slow smile. It was understandable he'd always been comfortable around Susannah, had from the time he was little. He was right to trust her then and now. To love her. For he did. Deeply. Heart swelling with emotion, he almost didn't hear his mother's words.

"You are besotted with her. Always have been, from the first time she came over to watch you when you were a *boppeli* and she a young girl. But you don't need a *kinder minder* now, Jethro, you need a wife who can give you a family."

Jethro found himself standing before he was aware of moving. He'd moved so quickly, the nearby Belgian jerked his head as high as the lead attached to his halter would allow, causing the post to which it was attached to creak in protest. Running a hand down the muscular neck, Jethro frowned as he saw his fingers were trembling. Sweeping his palm again against the horse's warm flesh, Jethro wasn't sure if the action was more calming to him or to the animal.

He wanted to keep his back to his mother. To reject what she was saying and maintain his attention on the gelding instead. But that wasn't the man he'd become. Pivoting, he saw she had also risen to her feet. "As you've said, I've t-turned out b-better without your help. I d-don't need it now in choosing who is right for m-me as a wife."

There was no hint of the earlier vulnerability in the woman who faced him. His *mamm* pursed her thin lips as she studied his face, as if weighing his resolve. Squaring his shoulders, Jethro met her gaze. His heart thudded as if he'd recently been the one in the harness pulling equipment instead of the Belgians. In fact, he'd rather put on the heavy horse collar and pull a plow across the field instead of engage in this confrontation. But he would if he had to. He'd endure anything he had to, if the reward was a life with Susannah.

His *mamm* didn't say another word. Dipping her chin slightly in acknowledgment, she turned and headed for the wide barn door. If her heavy stride was less than the confident one he'd previously known, it wasn't surprising. The conversation had probably been as wearying to her as it'd been to him. Possibly more so, as it seemed like a bottled-up lifetime had been uncorked in an abrupt moment.

Jethro bent to pick up the brush and rubber comb he'd dropped when he'd slid down the wall. What she'd shared wouldn't make any difference. It was his *mamm's* past. Whatever it was supposed to mean to him, one thing was clear: Susannah was his future. A future, for the first time, that he was looking forward to.

Tilting her head, Susannah put a hand on the wheel to stop the treadle sewing machine. *Ja.* There had been a knock at the door. With a distracted glance at the shirt she was making for Amos, she rose and walked across the large common room to the door. Her son was outgrowing his shirts as well as his pants every time she turned around. She might as well start cutting down some of Vernon's old clothes to see if they'd work to help keep up.

She'd packed them away for that possibility after he'd passed on. Which closet had she put them in? Running through the possibilities in her head, Susannah pulled open the door, a smile of greeting on her lips. But when she saw her visitor, Susannah wished she hadn't finished fall plowing earlier today. She'd rather be out in the field. Or in town running some errands. Anything would be better than facing the stern-jawed woman standing on the porch.

There was no need to guess what this visit would be about.

"Ruby," she greeted the bishop's wife flatly. "Won't you come in?"

Without a word, Jethro's *mamm* stepped into the house. Inhaling a girding breath, Susannah slowly closed the door behind her. *I'm a grown woman. Who loves a grown man who I think loves me. A man who doesn't need his parents' approval to marry. She can't quell the joy we shared together yesterday and that we can have in the future if we don't let her.*

"Would you like some *kaffi*?" Susannah gestured to the chairs by the table.

After only one step into the kitchen, Ruby confronted Susannah. "I want you to stop seeing my son. Stop putting ideas into his head about a relationship with you, when you are far from what he needs." The older woman cocked her head as her blue eyes tried to pin Susannah against the door.

"You're a *gut* woman, Susannah Mast. No doubt, you're hardworking, among many other qualities. I admire you. And I think you're a *gut* enough woman to know my son needs something different than the life you can give him. Sure and certain, you've always been *gut* with him. Right now, it might seem that marriage between the two of you would also be *gut*. That it would work. But what about a few years down the line? When your childbearing years are completely gone and his aren't? When he looks around at the families other men his age have. A family you would be keeping him from. Let him go." Her words, although quietly spoken, rang through the silent kitchen.

Ruby shook her head sadly. "You think I don't know my son? I do. He's lonely. He's lonely for more than just the companionship you can give him. He needs a family more than anyone I've ever known. A family you can't give him. It's true, I might not've done right by him. But I want to do right by him now. I'm asking you, as a mother, to help me do right by him now." Ruby lifted one of her hands, seemingly in supplication. It fell back to her side. The woman turned away, but not before Susannah thought she saw tears glistening in the woman's eyes. Surely that'd been a trick of the light through the window. Ruby Weaver...crying?

Susannah's rebuttal shriveled in her dry mouth. Anticipating this confrontation, she'd prepared herself for many arguments. But not how to respond to a mother's love in doing what she thought was best for her only son.

She loved Jethro. She wanted to marry him.

The relationship they had was unlike the companionable partnership she'd developed over the years with Vernon. *Ja*, this love had that, but it also had joy. Enthusiasm. Peace. Hope. Anticipation for the future. But was the anticipation all on her side? Like the early part of their mock courtship, was she thinking too much about how the relationship would benefit her and not what it would ultimately do to Jethro? Had he become too caught up, or perhaps even trapped, in the pretend that he felt he had to make it real? All of the reasons, good reasons, of why she'd earlier determined the relationship was foolish seeped back in through the cracks in her resolve that Jethro's mother had just created.

What would she want for Amos, should he be in the same position? Would she want him to marry a woman who possibly couldn't give him a family? Who couldn't give him a biological son or a daughter to inherit his own farm at some point? He'd already lost one child. She'd lost two. Unbidden, the image of an enthralled Jethro tenderly holding her infant grandson, Eli, filled her mind. Immediately joining it were memories of how patient he was with Amos. How good with Rebecca. Just because he would be a *wunderbar* husband for her didn't mean she'd be an equally *wunderbar* wife for him. She couldn't do that to Jethro. Not when she loved him.

Susannah suddenly felt so weary, like the residue after a dam had burst under the weight of an unusually heavy storm. *Maybe I am old.* Shuffling around Ruby, she crossed to the kitchen table and sank onto one of the chairs. With a bleak smile, she considered her unexpected guest as she repeated her earlier question. "Would you like some *kaffi*, Ruby?"

While she could defy the bishop's wife if the woman tried to badger her adult son, could stand in the way of anyone attempting to browbeat him, Susannah wouldn't argue with a mother who loved her child and wanted what was best for him. Not when she would do the same.

Chapter Seventeen

Jethro's eager stride slowed when Susannah stepped out of the barn. After the distressing interaction with his *mamm* today, he'd needed to see her. Even before the sound of his mother's horse's hoofbeats had faded away, Jethro had been counting the minutes until he could see Susannah as he'd hurried to finish up chores and other necessary tasks at his farm.

"Your *mamm* came to see me today."

Dread pooled in Jethro's stomach at Susannah's somber words. At her somber expression revealed even in the gathering dusk. His legs were filled with lead. He stopped— his breath, his heart, his gaze fixed on her face. Her closed-off expression. Jethro tried to swallow but his throat wouldn't cooperate. He should've come sooner. He should've gotten to Susannah before his mother had.

"D-don't listen t-to her." He was surprised he could get the words out through his stiff lips.

Wincing, Susannah shook her head. "But she made sense, Jethro."

"*Nee. We* m-make sense. The t-two of us t-together." How could he be so motionless when he was shaking to pieces inside?

She lowered her chin until, instead of her sorrowful brown eyes, he was facing the *kapp* pinned neatly to her brown hair. "*Nee.* We don't. I've lived a phase of my life that I can't get back for you, Jethro. You need someone who can go through that phase with you."

He lurched forward a step. "*Nee.* Let them say what they will, but I *know* what I need. I *know* the feelings I have for you." *Why does everyone think I can't feel? That I don't know my own mind? That they all know better? I'm a grown man. I've done what they wanted before. Am I not allowed to live my own life?* When Susannah lifted her head, his heart fell, as he could see in her pale, resolute face that, *nee*, in this, he wasn't allowed. At least not a life that would have Susannah in it as he'd dreamed.

This was so much harder even than she'd feared. Confronted by Jethro's desolate expression, Susannah was afraid she would shatter and blow away on the chilly October breeze. Or maybe the cold was all internal. If so, then she feared she'd be cold for a long, long time. Regardless of how much she wanted to respond to his entreaty, for him, she had to remain strong.

She shook her head. "You're mistaking the feelings you have for me for something else. You think it's…" She couldn't say *love*. If she used that word with him, it would be to tell him that she'd grown to love him more than she could ever have imagined. Which is why she had to do this. "It's comfort. What we have is a…comfortable companionship." Her throat was raw as she framed the words. What they had, what she felt they had, was so much more. But she could tell by his face that he wouldn't accept her decision unless she made him.

"You're imprinted on me, Jethro. Like a duckling. I gave you attention when you needed it, then and now, and we're—" she swallowed "—friends, and you've mistaken that for something else. That's all."

When he winced, she wanted to grab the words back.

"I thought you were so m-much m-more. I'd hoped you were so m-much m-more." His voice was hollow.

"You'll thank me later. We can still be friends."

His jaw clenched. "I d-don't need this kind of friendship. I can't d-do this kind of friendship."

"It's all we can have, Jethro." She couldn't stand it if they lost that connection as well as everything else. That'd been her fear from the beginning. If only they hadn't started down this charade! But if they hadn't, she wouldn't have the moments together she knew she'd treasure for the rest of her years. Closing the distance between them, she touched her hand to his dear, cherished face. "It's probable I can't give you a family." Her eyes squeezed shut for a moment at the memory of the two babies she'd lost. "You need a family."

She could feel his shuddering sigh through her fingers before he gently kissed their tips. "You'd b-be m-my family."

"Oh, Jethro." She smiled sadly as she lowered her hand, surreptitiously curling her fingers in to hold his kiss. "You think that now, but in ten years when I'm old and gray and you don't have anyone to inherit your farm, you'll think otherwise. You'll find a woman your age that would've worked out better for you and you'll regret that you were stuck with me."

"I'd never regret it. And Amos can farm it for m-me when he's grown."

"*Nee*, Jethro. This time, my answer is *nee* and it must remain so."

Gutted at her own words, Susannah wheeled and returned to the barn door on quavering legs. Slipping inside, she closed the door and hooked the latch before sagging against it. Face contorted, she remained propped there as she listened for sounds indicating the actions of the man on the other side. At last, she heard the retreating crunch of boots on gravel.

"Are you all right, *Mamm*?" Amos, his arms full of straw bedding for the stalls, was staring at her in concern.

Nee. She was anything but all right. But she would be. She had to be. It would just take time. Susannah feared it would be a long time.

"*Ja*," she assured him as she pushed upright. "It's just…been a long day."

With a doubtful nod, he continued on his way.

Moving away from the door, Susannah entered the first empty stall and crossed to the open window in time to watch Jethro's buggy travel down the lane. When even the glow of the orange caution triangle indicating a slow-moving vehicle faded from view, she turned from the window. And burst into tears. Not wanting to draw Amos's concerned attention again, she jerked open the barn door and stumbled through.

Once outside, she headed for the orchard. Her crying became unchecked. By the time she'd climbed up the hill in the light of the rising slivered moon and reached the trees, her head ached and her breath was coming in little hiccups.

"This is why I don't cry," she muttered through the thickness in her nose and throat. Lifting her apron, she dabbed at her eyes. *I did the right thing.* Jethro's face, his eyes so wounded, sprang into her mind. Tears began to leak anew. *Then why doesn't it feel like the right thing? Not for him, not for me. You're just thinking about now. You can't just think about now, you have to think about later, years later.* Slumping against the smooth trunk of one of the apple trees, the purported "years later" seemed empty and lonely as she wadded the serviceable cotton into a fist. But she could eventually find someone for companionship. She'd had companionship before.

Her mouth, numb from the crying, began to quiver. *Now I want love. Is that wrong? I did the right thing.* Maybe if she repeated it enough, she could finally accept it in her heart. *I did the right thing. I did the right thing.* It became a sob. One hand wrapped around her heaving stomach, Susannah used the other to wipe away the tears that made the thin moon just a blur.

Her breathing slowly quieted from hiccupping gasps to slow, steady breaths. Susannah tipped her head back against the tree. Another reason she didn't cry. For when she did, she was exhausted afterward, wrung out, like a dishrag that'd been twisted and squeezed. Emptied of everything. Like her heart...

Jethro didn't remember climbing back into the buggy. He didn't recall directing the gelding down the lane. Blinking distractedly, he realized they were headed toward the crossroad that would lead him to his own farm. Cocoa must've made the determination, as Jethro wasn't conscious of doing so. His gaze flicked momentarily to the side mirrors as the shapes of Susannah's and his parents' barns receded with every hoofbeat. At least the horse had turned away from his folks' farm. They were the last people he wanted to see right now.

What a fool he'd been. He'd allowed himself to hope. As he'd never really let himself want before, he'd had little cause for hope. Life had been a steady diet of disappointments. Disappointments that Jethro had thought were his due. But with Susannah, he'd hoped. Hoped that she'd love him for himself. Loved him in spite of himself. Loved the inner man even through his outer issues.

Why are you surprised when she didn't want you? She doesn't need another farm. She has a prosperous one. She doesn't need a tighter relationship with the district's bishop; she's already their closest neighbor, and regardless of their opinion on this, a respected one.

He fingered the lines. The gelding's ears flicked back in his direction, as if to ask him what he was thinking. Jethro's brow furrowed. His eyes narrowed as he stared ahead. *Susannah didn't need to agree with his parents to cultivate their good opinion. She frequently didn't agree. So why now?*

He saw not the starlit night with its fingernail moon but Susannah's pale face. Her rigid figure. Her glistening eyes. *Glistening? Susannah never cried.* Her hand against his mouth had been quivering. *Because she was mad? Nee. Because she'd been trying not to cry. Why would she want to cry? Because she didn't want to say what she was saying when she sent him away?* He scowled in disgust. *Why do I strive to hang on to some kind of hope?*

You're wallowing in your misery like a pig

in the mud, Jethro. Quit fooling yourself. Why continue to pursue a woman who doesn't want you? Like Louisa didn't, even when she had you.

But Susannah was different. If there was any possibility he could convince her to take a chance on them, wouldn't it be worth it? Just a chance, as small as a single stalk of straw in a full hayloft, that he could convince her to say yes, would he be a fool for not taking it? Jethro's jaw shifted as his teeth clenched.

Yes.

Oh, Lord, please don't let me make a mistake in this.

He'd spent a lifetime knowing his needs were always second to others. Second to Atlee's when he had come along. Second to his father's responsibilities as bishop. Second to Louisa's needs. Second to his mother's determination to be the bishop's wife she'd envisioned.

He needed Susannah. He needed her positive outlook. He needed her strength. He needed her acceptance. He needed her love. And he'd thought he had it. *Dear* Gott, *don't let me be wrong in that.*

He'd dated women his folks had directed him to. Even married one. If she'd lived, he'd have stayed married to Louisa for the rest of his days. But she hadn't. Was he going to let them chose a second one? *Gott* had given him a chance and he'd found love when *Gott* had dropped a buggy wreck on this very road. How many more chances would *Gott* give him if he turned his back on this one?

As for him needing a family, he'd have one with Susannah. He'd be proud to help raise Amos. Although a bit strange as Ben was near his age, he'd happily be *grossdaadi* to the twins, and any additional children Ben and Rachel, or for that matter, Rebecca and Amos whenever they married, would have. As everyone was so worried about him having a family, he'd found one he'd love to call his own.

Jethro drew the already confused gelding to a stop in the middle of the road. He loved his parents, he truly did. But as the *Biewel* said many times, a man shall leave his father and mother. It was time they let him. Let him make his own mistakes, if that's what this was.

But he knew it wasn't.

Resolute, he didn't even look for a field lane in which to turn the rig around. Looking both ways—there'd been too many buggy wrecks on this road as it was—Jethro ensured there were no lights from an oncoming car. Backing the gelding until the rear wheels of the buggy teetered into the far ditch, Jethro turned in the direction from which they'd come. The direction Jethro hoped would hold his future. A future he would choose. One with Susannah in it as his wife.

Eager to have the discussion with his parents that would free him for a better one with Susannah, he urged Cocoa to a greater pace. As the silhouettes of the farms came into view, Jethro leaned forward abruptly in the seat and asked the gelding for all the speed the horse possessed.

At the rapid staccato of hoofbeats, Susannah peeked through the branches to see a buggy racing down the road. Jethro's rig. Heading for his folks. To argue with them? Or agree?

As well as being a good man, Jethro was a good son. Although he might not agree with his parents in this, he would always honor them. *She had done the right thing.* Sniffing, Susannah wiped the remnants of tears from her face with her hand. She needed to get back to the barn and help Amos finish up chores. At least her nose had cleared enough that she could finally breathe again. With a deep sigh, she straightened from the trunk. A few strides later, she paused for another deep, exaggerated inhalation.

Was that smoke?

Stooping, she ripped up a handful of grass and tossed it into the air. As the fragments drifted across the orchard, she spun toward the opposing direction. The smell was stronger. Definitely smoke. The dark night quickly revealed the source. An orange glow haloed the bishop's house. Now that her eyes were on it, even across the large field that separated them, Susannah could see flames lick up one side of the building. Her legs were moving before she fully processed the sight.

"Amos! Amos!" she screamed as she sprinted for the barn. To her great relief, her son popped out of the barn door.

"Get the pony and race to the phone shack! Call the fire department and tell them Bishop Weaver's house is on fire!" Susannah dashed past where Amos stayed rooted, mouth agape. "Hurry!"

For a brief second, Susannah thought about grabbing Nutmeg and racing the mare the short stretch to the bishop's farm. Determining she could be at the Weaver's place before she could bridle the mare and later deal with the frightened animal around what was sure to be a dangerous situation, she pivoted for the lane.

In the distance, she heard the frightened whinny of a horse. The silhouette of Jethro's rig was visible as he rushed up the lane in front of the burning building. Susannah pumped her legs harder. Although he was a member of the local volunteer fire department and knew what actions to take, Jethro was alone. Alone at a fire in his parents' home. Were his parents inside?

Her heart was pounding. Energy fueled by adrenaline poured into her limbs as the fence posts between the farms flashed by in swift succession. Susannah couldn't feel her feet hitting the ground, but they must've been as she could hear the rapid slap of them on the blacktop. Her knees tangled in the confines of her skirt. Staggering, she almost went down before regaining her balance. Grabbing a handful of fabric, she jerked it up out of the way of her legs.

Halfway to the house she heard the clatter of the pony's hooves on the blacktop behind her, the sound barely discernible over her panting breath. Amos was on his way to call for help. Thank *Gott* he frequently raced the pony, even when she'd discouraged it. They'd make a fast trip to the phone shack.

The light surrounding the Weaver house had intensified. Now instead of just on one side, flames were creeping over the roof. Susannah frantically scanned the yard for any sign of figures in the fire's glow. *Jethro, where are you? Oh, don't go in alone! Where were the Weavers? Were they home?*

As Susannah swung into the lane, she saw that the buggy, pulled by the unfettered, spooked horse, had circled the farmyard and was heading back down the driveway toward her. Knowing the danger of a loose runaway with the impending traffic, Susannah staggered to halt in the middle of the lane. One hand on a trembling thigh, she stretched out the other to stop the frightened animal. To her relief, the horse skidded to a standstill a few feet from her. Susannah snagged the rein just under the bit and stroked a hand along the gelding's sweaty neck.

"That's a boy," she soothed between pants. Scanning the area, Susannah searched for a place the horse would be safe. With a gentle tug on the rein, she trotted the skittish animal across the blacktop to a field entrance. Ensuring the rig was well clear of the road, she secured him to a post that supported a field gate. Breathing nearly recovered, she raced back across the road. Her steps slowed to an appalled walk up the lane.

The fire's crackle and pop made it almost seem alive. Orange flames assaulted the house from multiple locations. Shades of smoke rose up into the sky. Susannah felt like she was caught between two dimensions. Searing heat flushed her skin that faced the fire. The dropping temperature chilled the side away from it.

Mesmerized by the horrifying sight before her, Susannah at first didn't separate the sound from the fire's ominous rumbling. When she recognized that whatever it was, it wasn't of the fire, she frantically searched the yard. Several heart-pounding seconds later, she located a dark shape on the ground, yards from the front door. Cringing against the hostile heat, she rushed to the figure.

The bishop lay on his back, his lanky legs bent at the knees. His chest rose and fell with wheezes interspersed with harsh coughing. The man's gray hair was in tangled disarray around his hatless head. His face was slick with sweat.

"We have to get farther away. Can you move?" Susannah bent to grab his arm.

"*Ja*," he wheezed. "I think so." He struggled up on his elbows to stare with a shattered expression at his home.

"Come on," Susannah urged. With a hand on his forearm, Susannah propelled him to his feet. As a clumsy team, they staggered step-by-step until the gravel of the driveway was under her feet. She kept him upright until they'd crossed the grass on the driveway's far side. Hoping they'd come far enough, for now at least, she helped the bishop sink down next to the water trough that served as part of the livestock enclosure.

"Where's Jethro? Where's Ruby?" she gasped.

The bishop's face was white in the flickering light of the fire. "He went back in to get her."

Chapter Eighteen

❧

Susannah jerked upright to stare at the front door of the house. The fire had taken possession from when they were outside it only moments before. Flames flared through the nearby window. In the glow, the house's white paint pocked with blisters. She choked on a sharp inhalation, smoke and despair clogging her throat.

Jethro was in the burning house.

A dark blur darted across the yard. Jethro? Or were her eyes, beleaguered with tears and smoke, playing tricks on her? Was it Ruby? The figure in the erratic shadows turned, exposing a pale face. Susannah launched herself toward it. She shrieked and stumbled when a small explosion rocked the night. Flying glass and debris burst from a side window, knocking the figure down.

Staggering to regain her footing, Susannah focused her attention on the downed body. The fire roared a victory after the blast. *Oh, please, please let Jethro be all right!* At the faint whine of a siren, she whimpered in relief. A quick glance revealed a pulsing blue light that penetrated the night sky beyond her farm. Her strides diminished to a jarring halt as she neared the motionless figure. It was too small to be Jethro. Too short to be Ruby. Who then? She dropped to her knees beside it.

The slender chest was wracked with coughing. When the body jerked with laboring breath, Susannah helped it turn to the side. She gasped at the sight of John Schlabach's grimy, gaunt face.

"Are you hurt? Can you get up? We have to get out of here!" she yelled over the rumbling behind her.

The house groaned as if complaining when its interior began giving way under the onslaught of the flames. Susannah's stomach churned at the sound. At her ex-hired hand's feeble nod, she jerked him up, pulling him away from the now fully engaged house even before he completely regained his feet. As they crossed the driveway in a staggering run, Susannah prayed she wasn't doing further damage to any injuries the boy might've sustained in the blast. When they reached the pasture fence, she braced him against the boards.

"Did they get out?" Susannah barely heard the words interspersed in John's coughing and wheezing. "Are they all right?" He bent over at the waist as he panted. Susannah placed a light hand on his back in support. Under her fingers, she could feel the ridges of his spine. Her eyes, burning from the smoke, closed in despair. Where was Jethro? Was he out? Was he safe? Torn with the need to search for the man she loved, to scan for any sign of him, she remained instead with the boy who needed her.

The sound of sirens battled with the roar of the fire and the crash of shattering glass. Occasionally a shrill whinny from a frightened horse—the one she'd secured across the road and ones in the barn—were discernible. Susannah wanted to weep with relief when Gabe Bartel's pickup swept into the lane. As John was now standing upright beside her, she waved the local EMS provider on to where she'd left the bishop. And Jethro? Were he and his mother out of the house? *Oh, please,* Gott, *let them be out.*

Distant sirens indicated more help was on the way. Would they be too late? Or was it too late for her and Jethro to have any chance at a future? If he were only safe, Susannah would happily spend the rest of her life as his wife, if that's what he wanted. Regardless of what others thought best. When her son loved like she loved, she wouldn't stand in his way.

John was crying. Tears tracked from his bloodshot eyes over his grimy cheeks to drip off his chin. "I only wanted to hurt them a little. Hurt them like they hurt my *daed*. The bishop and the ministers drove him away. If they hadn't done that, things would've been better. He wouldn't have left. He wouldn't have died like he did."

Susannah cringed at the mumbled words. She didn't know what to say. The boy was seeing a version of reality that existed only in his mind. But a child longs to love his parents. She wrapped her arms around John's shoulders and drew his thin, unresisting frame to her.

"What if I've killed them? I didn't mean to kill them. I just wanted someone to hurt like I hurt." The boy gasped in air between sobs. "I kept thinking he'd come back and he'd be different and it would be all right. We'd be a family again."

Hot tears dripped against her neck. Were they John's, or hers? Susannah didn't know. She didn't care. The only thing she cared about was seeing Jethro emerge from the growing inferno a short distance away. John shuddered in her arms. *Ach, nee.* She cared about this troubled boy. And what might become of him. How incredibly disheartening if Mervin Schlabach destroyed another life beyond his own.

Susannah stroked gentle fingers through the youth's grimy hair. "For all have sinned and fallen short of the glory of God, John. It's normal to want to love your parents. *Gott* wants you to love your parents. But sometimes parents don't always make the best choices. For themselves, or for their children," she murmured. "You're not your father, John. Confession is well on the path to repentance. You can determine your life going forward. *Gott* can change it. We are here to help you."

Vehicles bearing the emblem of the Miller's Creek volunteer fire department roared up the lane. Doors slammed as men launched from vehicles. Susannah shifted with the trembling boy she supported until she could look back toward the livestock trough where she'd left the bishop.

Her arms sagged from around John's frame when she saw not one but three figures beyond the EMT garbed in his bulky reflective gear. One of them was on the ground, leaning against the bishop, the face partially covered by an oxygen mask. The other was standing, facing her direction. Slight steam vapors wafted from him. Stunned, Susannah watched as Gabe draped one wet towel around the man's neck and another over the top of his head. Then she burst into tears.

John glanced up at her in surprise before he, too, looked in that direction. His body began quaking again with sobs. "I didn't kill them. I'm so thankful I didn't kill them."

Flashing lights and sirens intensified as more trucks parked along the lane when fire departments from other towns arrived to join the fight.

Susannah's gaze remained locked on the man draped in towels. He took a step in her direction before Gabe stopped him with raised hand. The EMT rose from where he'd been attending the Weavers and turned his full attention to the one who'd saved them.

Jethro was alive.

Susannah's legs gave out. If it hadn't been for John, she would've crumpled to the ground. At the touch on her shoulder, she twisted to see David Neuenschwander, one of the Amish volunteer firefighters, beside them.

"I've got John." Under his helmet, a smile was evident on the older man's kindly face. "Why don't you go see if Gabe needs any help?"

Susannah nodded mutely. Through the ashes

that drifted down between them, she saw the bishop struggle to his feet. He stumbled over to wrap his arms around his son. Jethro wobbled under the embrace, but his father held him steady. His attention on her approach, Jethro tipped his head to something the bishop must've spoken. He said something back before patting the older man's shoulder. With a nod, Ezekiel lowered his arms and settled back down beside his wife.

Susannah's heart lurched as, without breaking eye contact, Jethro started in her direction. A few coughs punctuated his progress, but his arms were as strong as Susannah could ever hope for when they wrapped around her. She even relished the heavy smell of smoke that permeated the shirt under her nose, as she could feel the powerful beat of his heart beneath it.

"I was so afraid." She breathed the words. "I didn't see you. When I heard the explosion…" Burrowing deeper into his embrace, she tightened her arms around the waist that was damp with sweat and the towels that still draped him.

"We couldn't get to the front d-door. *Gut* thing, as the small p-propane tank that feeds the lamp blew right when we would've passed it. We went out through the mudroom into the side yard."

"Your *mamm*?"

"She's all right."

Susannah's face contorted in relief as tears leaked anew. She flinched at the crash of timbers behind her, but now the roar of the fire was accompanied with the hiss of the water beginning to suppress it. Safe in Jethro's arms, she took in the surreal scene in the normally tranquil farmyard. Red and blue lights flashed, highlighting the safety stripes on the gear worn by the men who were spread over the property manning fire hoses. Although the house couldn't be saved, they were ensuring none of the other buildings were caught up in the inferno.

"Are you truly all right?"

"*Ja*. Gabe checked me over p-pretty *gut*. For smoke inhalation, b-burns, heat exhaustion. Wouldn't let m-me come t-to you until he d-did so." She felt a kiss against her hair. "B-but he couldn't stop me from coming t-to you, Susannah. Nothing could stop me. You b-better get used t-to it. I'll always come t-to you."

Smiling, Susannah looked into his dear, dear face. "Do you remember when you asked me about the qualities I'd look for in a husband? I just realized that persistence is a very important one. In fact, I've been doing a lot of consideration lately regarding the qualities

I'd look for in a mate. I'm still not sure what all they are, but it doesn't matter, as the mate I'd been looking for was you."

Jethro's arms flexed around her. "*Gut* thing. As I've known m-mine was you for a long t-time." His heavy sigh, although interspersed with a few coughs, was heartfelt. "I'm sure one of the qualities wasn't a stutter."

"Jethro, I never hear the stutter. I just hear you." Her gaze rested on the bedraggled couple huddled together by the trough under Gabe's watchful eye.

"What about your folks, Jethro? Are you all right without their approval?"

"I have it. We have it." His smile flashed white in his soot-covered face. "I was willing t-to give m-my life for them. I can surely be t-trusted to m-make a *gut* decision who b-best to spend that life with."

"They're right in that I can't give you children or a family. My only value to contribute is the farm."

"What's your farm got t-to d-do with us? I d-don't want you for your farm. I want you. In fact, you can d-deed the farm over to Amos right now if you wish. Or anyone else, for that m-matter. As for a family, you're my family. Your children will be my family. I can't imagine one I'd want m-more."

Susannah closed her eyes against the surrounding chaos and opened them to see only the man who held her. A man she couldn't imagine wanting more, either.

Epilogue

Jethro's hand tightened on Susannah's as they sauntered up the hill to the orchard. The moonlight reflecting on the snow in the clear night was all the light they needed. Even though the cold November temperature nipped at her nose, she was happy to forego her gloves to feel the hand enfolding hers.

The apple trees, their branches draped in a light snow, were dormant for the winter. Susannah looked from their frail skeletons to the one far across the field of Bishop Weaver's house. Although the fire had rapidly been controlled, between it and the resulting water damage, little in the house had been salvageable. The district had promptly rallied to provide the bishop and his wife with everything they might need.

Initially, the couple had moved into the

apartment in town above The Stitch quilt shop, recently vacated by Hannah and Gabe Bartle. For the rest of this winter, at least, they were moving into Jethro's house. His place was now with Susannah, his wife.

"Do you think they'll move back here again in the spring? The community would certainly build a house for them."

"I d-don't know. It depends how my *mamm* would feel about it at the t-time. It makes her... uncomfortable t-to have the district continually p-providing for her."

"We could build a *daadi haus* and have them move in here."

Jethro stared at her as if he'd never heard of the term for the onsite residence that housed the older Amish generation.

"You would let m-my p-parents, m-my *m-mamm*, m-move in right next d-door?"

"Why not? They've been my neighbors all my life. And they're your parents. They are always welcome. Although we won't have grandchildren for them." She worried her lip before drawing in a deep breath. "Are you sure you won't regret that?"

"We've gone over that. M-my only regret would be in not sharing every m-moment of m-my life that I p-possibly can with you."

Susannah sighed, comforted more than she

could say by his words. And so glad that his life hadn't ended on that night.

The bishop hadn't pressed charges against John. As was their way, he forgave the remorseful youth, working instead with the authorities to release the boy on probation into his mother's care. With some additional guiding influences.

Stroking his thumb in slow circles over the back of Susannah's hand, Jethro seemed to read her thoughts. "I'd heard the old b-boy, D-David Neuenschwander, will no longer be an old b-boy when he m-marries Lavinia Schlabach. Seems the new matchmaker had something to d-do with that."

Smiling, Susannah tipped her head back to take in the brilliance of the stars overhead in the crisp clear night. "I'm glad for him. I'm glad for them all. He's a gentle, patient man. I figured, if those qualities would do well for a troubled horse, they might help a troubled boy as well. And a woman who'd waited a long time for a *gut* man. It was just a matter of getting them together to see it themselves."

"I think their courtship surprised everyone."

"More so than ours?"

Jethro grinned. "If anyone had p-paid any attention to the way I looked at you, they wouldn't have b-been surprised."

"Well, I was surprised." She lifted their joined hands to her cheek, where she rested his chilled fingers against it before turning her head to place a soft kiss on them. "In the best way." She thought about the misunderstanding that'd temporarily broken them up. "You spoke with Mrs. Danvers regarding your speech?"

"*Ja.* B-but I won't b-be working with her. I wouldn't have chosen this, b-but it's who I am. She d-did suggest some t-tools to help me relax when speaking that will improve the stuttering. I'm relaxed with you. See, it's better all ready. B-because if you're content, I'm content." Releasing her hand, he tucked her against him as he wrapped his arms around her.

Leaning back against his chest, Susannah rested her hands on the ones clasped at her waist. "I'm content. I'm so much more than content."

"I walked with a woman here once who t-told me she was t-too old for romance. Is she still t-too old?"

"*Nee.* Never. Maybe I just never knew what it was."

"I'm glad I, of all p-people, got to be the one t-to show you."

"Romance," she mused. "Well, that might be a quality in a spouse I wouldn't have looked for—" she entwined her fingers with his "—but I'm glad my husband has it."

"I l-l-love you."

Pulling out of his arms, Susannah turned to meet his gaze, her eyes widened with awe before they narrowed with concern. Jethro had never struggled with that letter before. When she saw the breadth of his smile, she relaxed.

"For the first t-time in m-my life I'm glad for the stutter. I've never t-told anyone I loved them b-before. I wanted to linger over the words."

He kissed her. And he lingered over that as well.

* * * * *

Dear Reader,

Sometimes when writing a story, a character pops up out of the blue. You didn't expect them. You didn't plan for them. But they touch you and you can't forget them. Jethro was one of those characters. He showed up unexpectedly in the second Miller's Creek book, *Amish Reckoning*. By the time I'd written *Her Forbidden Amish Love*, I knew I wanted to get to know him better. And readers would, too.

Some people might be like that in our lives. They show up unexpectedly, you want to get to know them better, and they end up playing an important part in your life. Maybe temporarily. Maybe for a lifetime. Sometimes just when you need them. I've had folks like that in my life. I hope I meet many more.

Thanks so much for choosing to read Jethro and Susannah's story. To keep updated on what might be next, stop by jocelynmcclay.com or visit me on Facebook.

God Bless You,
Jocelyn McClay

Get 4 FREE REWARDS!

We'll send you 2 FREE Books plus 2 FREE Mystery Gifts.

FREE Value Over $20

Both the **Love Inspired®** and **Love Inspired® Suspense** series feature compelling novels filled with inspirational romance, faith, forgiveness, and hope.

YES! Please send me 2 FREE novels from the Love Inspired or Love Inspired Suspense series and my 2 FREE gifts (gifts are worth about $10 retail). After receiving them, if I don't wish to receive any more books, I can return the shipping statement marked "cancel." If I don't cancel, I will receive 6 brand-new Love Inspired Larger-Print books or Love Inspired Suspense Larger-Print books every month and be billed just $5.99 each in the U.S. or $6.24 each in Canada. That is a savings of at least 17% off the cover price. It's quite a bargain! Shipping and handling is just 50¢ per book in the U.S. and $1.25 per book in Canada. I understand that accepting the 2 free books and gifts places me under no obligation to buy anything. I can always return a shipment and cancel at any time. The free books and gifts are mine to keep no matter what I decide.

Choose one: ☐ **Love Inspired**
Larger-Print
(122/322 IDN GNWC)

☐ **Love Inspired Suspense**
Larger-Print
(107/307 IDN GNWN)

Name (please print)

Address   Apt. #

City   State/Province   Zip/Postal Code

Email: Please check this box ☐ if you would like to receive newsletters and promotional emails from Harlequin Enterprises ULC and its affiliates. You can unsubscribe anytime.

Mail to the Harlequin Reader Service:
IN U.S.A.: P.O. Box 1341, Buffalo, NY 14240-8531
IN CANADA: P.O. Box 603, Fort Erie, Ontario L2A 5X3

Want to try 2 free books from another series? Call 1-800-873-8635 or visit www.ReaderService.com.

*Terms and prices subject to change without notice. Prices do not include sales taxes, which will be charged (if applicable) based on your state or country of residence. Canadian residents will be charged applicable taxes. Offer not valid in Quebec. This offer is limited to one order per household. Books received may not be as shown. Not valid for current subscribers to the Love Inspired or Love Inspired Suspense series. All orders subject to approval. Credit or debit balances in a customer's account(s) may be offset by any other outstanding balance owed by or to the customer. Please allow 4 to 6 weeks for delivery. Offer available while quantities last.

Your Privacy—Your information is being collected by Harlequin Enterprises ULC, operating as Harlequin Reader Service. For a complete summary of the information we collect, how we use this information and to whom it is disclosed, please visit our privacy notice located at corporate.harlequin.com/privacy-notice. From time to time we may also exchange your personal information with reputable third parties. If you wish to opt out of this sharing of your personal information, please visit readerservice.com/consumerschoice or call 1-800-873-8635. **Notice to California Residents**—Under California law, you have specific rights to control and access your data. For more information on these rights and how to exercise them, visit corporate.harlequin.com/california-privacy.

LIRLIS22

Get 4 FREE REWARDS!

We'll send you 2 FREE Books plus 2 FREE Mystery Gifts.

FREE Value Over **$20**

Both the **Harlequin® Special Edition** and **Harlequin® Heartwarming™** series feature compelling novels filled with stories of love and strength where the bonds of friendship, family and community unite.

YES! Please send me 2 FREE novels from the Harlequin Special Edition or Harlequin Heartwarming series and my 2 FREE gifts (gifts are worth about $10 retail). After receiving them, if I don't wish to receive any more books, I can return the shipping statement marked "cancel." If I don't cancel, I will receive 6 brand-new Harlequin Special Edition books every month and be billed just $4.99 each in the U.S or $5.74 each in Canada, a savings of at least 17% off the cover price or 4 brand-new Harlequin Heartwarming Larger-Print books every month and be billed just $5.74 each in the U.S. or $6.24 each in Canada, a savings of at least 21% off the cover price. It's quite a bargain! Shipping and handling is just 50¢ per book in the U.S. and $1.25 per book in Canada.* I understand that accepting the 2 free books and gifts places me under no obligation to buy anything. I can always return a shipment and cancel at any time. The free books and gifts are mine to keep no matter what I decide.

Choose one: ☐ **Harlequin Special Edition** ☐ **Harlequin Heartwarming**
(235/335 HDN GNMP)   **Larger-Print**
(161/361 HDN GNPZ)

Name (please print)

Address   Apt. #

City   State/Province   Zip/Postal Code

Email: Please check this box ☐ if you would like to receive newsletters and promotional emails from Harlequin Enterprises ULC and its affiliates. You can unsubscribe anytime.

Mail to the **Harlequin Reader Service:**
IN U.S.A.: P.O. Box 1341, Buffalo, NY 14240-8531
IN CANADA: P.O. Box 603, Fort Erie, Ontario L2A 5X3

Want to try 2 free books from another series! Call 1-800-873-8635 or visit www.ReaderService.com.

*Terms and prices subject to change without notice. Prices do not include sales taxes, which will be charged (if applicable) based on your state or country of residence. Canadian residents will be charged applicable taxes. Offer not valid in Quebec. This offer is limited to one order per household. Books received may not be as shown. Not valid for current subscribers to the Harlequin Special Edition or Harlequin Heartwarming series. All orders subject to approval. Credit or debit balances in a customer's account(s) may be offset by any other outstanding balance owed by or to the customer. Please allow 4 to 6 weeks for delivery. Offer available while quantities last.

Your Privacy—Your information is being collected by Harlequin Enterprises ULC, operating as Harlequin Reader Service. For a complete summary of the information we collect, how we use this information and to whom it is disclosed, please visit our privacy notice located at corporate.harlequin.com/privacy-notice. From time to time we may also exchange your personal information with reputable third parties. If you wish to opt out of this sharing of your personal information, please visit readerservice.com/consumerchoice or call 1-800-873-8635. **Notice to California Residents**—Under California law, you have specific rights to control and access your data. For more information on these rights and how to exercise them, visit corporate.harlequin.com/california-privacy.

HSEHW22

LICNM0222